Rainbow Sprinkles

LITTLE CAKES, BOOK ONE

PEPPER NORTH

PAIGE MICHAELS

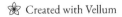 Created with Vellum

About the Book

Welcome to Little Cakes, the bakery that plays Daddy matchmaker! Little Cakes is a sweet and satisfying series, but dare to taste only if you like delicious Daddies, luscious Littles, and guaranteed happily-ever-afters.

Ellie Wilmoth has dreamed of owning her own cupcake bakery. Now that Little Cakes is about to open, nothing can distract her. Okay, maybe one thing. While crafting her first featured cupcake, she's interrupted by her handsome new landlord, and his commanding presence is impossible to ignore.

Garrett Erickson is enchanted by the sprinkle-covered, sugar-fueled woman renting his property. When he discovers her alone behind an unlocked door in the predawn darkness, his protective instincts won't be ignored. Is it possible she's the Little he's been looking for?

Prologue

"I can't believe it's finally happening," Ellie exclaimed as she spun around in a circle, taking in the space she'd just rented.

"We did it," Lark responded as she tucked the lease papers back into her briefcase. "It's official. Knowing how passionate and hardworking you are, Little Cakes will be open for business in no time."

Ellie couldn't stop grinning as she faced the front windows. "I'm going to put the most amazing cupcake display in front of the windows." She turned to the right. "And this wall can have cute gifts." She spun a one eighty. "And little tables and chairs over there..."

Lark laughed. "You have it all figured out. I know it's going to be fabulous. I can't wait to try all your cupcakes." She patted her stomach. "I'm gaining weight just thinking about it."

Ellie giggled and clapped her hands together before rushing over to give her friend a hug. "I can't thank you enough for helping me find the space."

"Well, I am a realtor, and you are one of my best friends, so..."

Ellie leaned back, still holding her friend's shoulders.

"You're still the best, and I appreciate everything you did to make this possible."

Lark smiled, her voice dipping. "I'm still sorry about your grandmother's passing, but I know she would be tickled to find out you're making your dreams come true with your inheritance."

Ellie nodded. She hated that her grandmother was gone. The woman had raised her from the time she was five, when her mother took off and never returned. For twenty-five years, it had been Ellie and her grandmother against the world. Now, Ellie had no living relatives, but she knew her grandmother would be so proud of her.

It was all coming together. Ellie had quit her job working as a pastry chef in one of the local exclusive hotels and taken the plunge.

In a few short days, Little Cakes would be open for business.

Chapter One

"Little Cakes, Little Cakes, we should all eat Little Cakes," Ellie sang at the top of her lungs to the music playing in the background as she twirled around the giant kitchen. "Pink and blue, red and green, it's all about delicious frosting…"

Suddenly, a large presence caught her attention, looming in the doorway to the back section of her store. She screamed, flinching so hard at the same time the cup of flour in her hands went flying into the air all around her.

The man rushed forward. "I'm so sorry. I didn't mean to frighten you."

Eyes wide, she backed up so fast she almost fell from slipping on the flour-covered floor. "Who are you?"

"Garrett Erickson. I own the building. I'm terribly sorry. I assume you're Ellie Willmoth." He stopped advancing and pointed over his broad shoulder. "I knocked several times, but you couldn't hear me over the music."

Ellie was breathing heavily as she flattened her hand over her chest. "You scared me to death." She reached over to turn off the music coming from her cell phone.

"My apologies." His expression was sincere. She had to give him that. And she recognized his name. She hadn't met Garrett

Erickson yet, but she knew he owned the strip mall where she was renting her space. He was tall with dark hair that was graying at the edges. So handsome. Piercing green eyes she could get lost in.

He glanced around. "I saw the lights coming from the back of the shop and was worried. What are you doing here at two in the morning?"

She took a deep breath to slow her racing heart rate. "Baking, of course. I'm planning to open next week. I'm still experimenting."

"In the middle of the night?"

She shrugged. "I lost track of time. I do that when I get in the groove."

He glanced around her space again before facing her. His expression was curious, a combination of a smirk and a frown. His brows were furrowed as if he were about to lecture her, but his lips were lifted as if he might chuckle instead.

And what was she thinking? Lecture her? He didn't know her well enough to comment on the hours she worked. It wasn't as if she was not permitted to work in her store any hour of the day or night she pleased.

He continued forward until he stood across from her on the other side of the island where she'd been mixing her next batch of cupcakes. "Are you always this...messy?"

Her back stiffened, and she straightened her spine so that she stood at her full height of five-three, while he had to be six foot. She brushed a stray lock of hair from her face, realizing not much of her thick, shoulder-length, brown hair was still secured in the ponytail she had gathered high on her head. "I prefer to call myself creative," she stated defensively.

His smirk grew into a legit smile. "Do you now?" He trailed a finger through the sugar she'd spilled all over the counter earlier.

She rushed forward, feeling less fearful now that her heart was no longer pounding out of her chest. She snagged a cupcake from one end of the counter and handed it to him. "Try it."

On second thought, her heart kicked up a notch when she met his gaze again. The grin on his face and the twinkle in his eyes made her panties dampen, shocking her. How had she gone from freaking out over finding a stranger in her shop to panting over him in so few minutes?

He held the cupcake, twisting it around in circles. "You're very good at what you do, I'll give you that. Every one of them looks exactly perfect. You like colorful things, don't you?" he teased.

She bit the corner of her bottom lip as she glanced at the confections scattered on her counter. Pink, purple, yellow, blue... "Yeah."

"What do you call this one?"

"Rainbow Sprinkles."

He chuckled. "Apropos. What flavor is it?"

"Rainbow," she declared, unable to keep from smiling back at him.

Another laugh. "Rainbow isn't a flavor."

"Sure it is. Are you just going to stare at it or eat it?"

"I don't think I've ever eaten a cupcake in the middle of the night."

She rolled her eyes. "I figured. You don't look like you eat many cupcakes at any time of the day. Live a little. Lightening won't strike. I promise."

His laugh made her shiver from head to toe. He finally peeled the wrapper back and took a generous bite. When he moaned as his eyes rolled back, she stopped breathing. The sound burrowed into her. Deep baritone. So sexy.

She gripped the edge of the counter as she watched him lick frosting from his lips.

"Damn, that's good."

She beamed. "Glad you like it."

He pointed at the mixing bowl in front of her. "What are you concocting now?"

"Lemon chiffon."

"When do you sleep?"

She shrugged. "When I get tired. I've been hyper and excited and exhilarated since I secured this space. I want to make a huge impression when I open."

He set the rest of the cupcake down on the counter and slowly rounded to her side, seeming to take in the entire kitchen. As he got closer to her, she swallowed. His proximity might make her faint.

Why did he have to be so freaking attractive? He wasn't a prospective boyfriend. He was the owner of her building. He was humoring her. Or more likely making sure she was taking care of her rented space properly.

When he rounded the counter, he stopped, his gaze roaming up and down her body from head to toe and back again. Slowly.

Her face heated when his easy smile turned into more of a smirk, and she glanced down to remind herself what she was wearing.

Shit. She sucked in a breath. She had on a white tank top, her favorite flannel pants covered in colorful cupcakes, and cupcake slippers. The huge, bulky, fluffy kind. Good grief.

"Cute," he stated. She couldn't read into that one word. Was he making fun of her?

She straightened her spine again and set her hands on her hips, undoubtedly pushing her ample chest outward. She wasn't a tiny gal. She had curves. She made cupcakes for a living. And she enjoyed them. With curves came boobs. At least she was wearing a bra tonight. Sometimes she got tired of the underwires and took them off while she was working.

He held up both hands. "Don't get defensive. I didn't mean to offend you. I genuinely like your style. Carefree. Fun. Especially the slippers." He winked at her.

She narrowed her gaze. "If you're making fun of me..."

He shook his head. "Nope. Never." He stepped closer until only inches separated them. And then he reached up and swiped at her cheek. "You have flour on your face." He grinned and then brought his finger to his mouth and sucked it. "Or maybe it's powdered sugar."

Her breath hitched. He had her completely flustered. The only times she felt this unsettled were when she was at the club meeting a Daddy Dom for the first time.

Ellie grabbed a cloth from the counter and swiped at her face, probably making it worse.

Garrett pointed at her phone, the corner of his mouth tipping up yet again. "What was that you were singing when I came in?"

She flushed a deep shade of red she could feel all the way to her bones. "Nothing. I made it up," she mumbled.

He chuckled. "It was cute. Something about cupcakes and frosting."

"I was just being silly."

"But you like youthful musical tunes."

She shrugged, not meeting his gaze as she busied herself, uselessly trying to wipe off the far end of the counter. "They make me happy."

"Nothing wrong with that." After an awkward moment of silence, he continued. "Do you always work in the middle of the night like this?"

"Not always. Only when I'm too hyped up to sleep. Might as well be working." She kept wiping the counter, though she was only managing to push flour around.

"It's not safe for you to be here alone like this," he pointed out.

She lifted her head and rolled her eyes, blurting out the first thing that popped into her mind without thinking. "Okay, Daddy." She even added an enormous amount of snark and less than a second later gasped, her eyes going wide.

His eyes were wide, too.

She gulped, racing to fix her faux pas. "Shit. Sorry. That came out wrong."

He chuckled. "Did it?"

"Yes, of course," she rushed to add. "Thank you for the advice. I'm a grown woman. I think I can take care of myself." Once again, she forced herself to stand taller, realizing it had to be impossible to take her seriously as said grown woman while wearing silly slippers and bright flannel pants.

He reached for her chin and tipped her head back, his brows furrowed. "I'm serious, Ellie. You shouldn't be working alone in the dark like this. Do you have someone who can be here with you? A boyfriend? Husband?"

She swallowed. Was he fishing for information about her marital and dating status? Surely not. "Don't need a man. I'm capable of taking care of myself."

He held her chin and her gaze for a moment before releasing her to reach into his back pocket and pulling out a business card, setting it on the island. "If you must be here at night, and you don't have anyone to ensure your safety, call me. Will you do that?"

Not a chance. "Thanks for the offer. That's very kind of you." Her knees were shaking.

"Ellie... Even if I thought you had ten years of self-defense classes, you're still just a slip of a woman. Anyone could over-power you in seconds."

She took a step back and crossed her arms. She was hardly a slip of a woman. How ridiculous.

"You're not going to call, are you?"

"Probably not," she admitted.

"Then I'll just have to drive by here every night to make sure you're safe."

She dropped her shoulders. "Gah. Fine. I'll call. Happy?" She had no idea where this bratty side was coming from. Well, that wasn't entirely true. She could be bratty. That wasn't a problem. But she didn't usually let any aspect of her Little peek out in inappropriate situations.

This situation was definitely inappropriate. She needed to get rid of Garrett. She'd already made several blunders, including casually calling him Daddy. She shuddered.

His face returned to that slightly jovial look. "Aren't you snarky?" He narrowed his gaze. "Have I seen you somewhere before?"

"Not that I know of." She prayed he wasn't a member of Blaze, her favorite local fetish club. She would absolutely die if he was. But it wasn't likely because she wouldn't have missed him if she'd seen him at the club. He was tall, dark, and handsome. Perfect Daddy material. He would have made her do a doubletake.

"Hmm. Well, are you almost done? Can I walk you to your car?"

"I walked here. I just live a few blocks away."

She shouldn't have said that. Ugh.

"You were planning to walk home in the middle of the night?" Yep. His expression was back to full-on Daddy face, and she had the sudden vision of him taking her over his knee and spanking her for endangering her life. Wouldn't that make her swoon? The image alone was doing crazy things to her libido.

"Uhh... Maybe?"

He shook his head. "Not a chance. How much longer will you be? I'll wait for you."

"You don't have to do that, Sir." She winced inwardly after calling him Sir.

He lifted one brow. "Oh, I definitely do."

She sighed. "Fine. I'll wrap things up." She reached for the dry ingredients she'd been putting in the mixer and snapped a lid over the top. It would be fine until tomorrow. Next, she put all the cupcakes she'd made so far in the refrigerator.

When she turned around, Garrett was cleaning off the counter.

"You don't have to do that either, S—" She sucked in a breath, coming far too close to calling him Sir again. What was wrong with her? Why was she getting such strong Daddy vibes from this man who was the owner of her building?

It wouldn't even matter if he was a Daddy. It would be extremely inappropriate for her to start a relationship with the owner of the strip mall. Besides, she had to be reading too much into his words and actions.

"I know I don't. But I'm not going to just stand here and watch you clean." Garrett washed out the cloth and started again. There really was a lot of flour and sugar on the counter. Tidy wasn't her middle name.

As soon as he had his back to her, she planted her gaze on his fantastic ass. His glutes and thighs flexed as he worked, making her salivate. Even though she wasn't exactly a stick figure, he would easily be able to handle her. The thought of him holding her over his lap crept in unwanted again.

It had been a few weeks since she'd last visited Blaze. She was jonesing for a night at the club, a night where she could indulge her Little side without judgment. Withdrawal was warping her perception of her interactions with this total stranger.

As she swept the floor, trying not to look at Garrett any more than necessary, she promised herself she would take the time this weekend to go to the club. It would do her good and help her relax. Lord knew she'd been crazy hyper the last several weeks leading up to her grand opening.

"Ready?" he asked as she tucked the broom back in the closet.

She spun around. "Sure. Just let me get my shoes." She grabbed her hot pink backpack from a hook along the wall and dropped onto a chair to put her tennis shoes on and store her slippers in the bag. "Wait..." she said as she rose to her feet. "You're so worried about a stranger attacking me. How do I know you are who you say you are? What if you're an imposter and now I'm going to lead you straight to my apartment? You'll know where I live. You could come back and kill me later in the night."

He didn't laugh. "You're absolutely right." He pointed at his card still sitting on the counter and then pulled out his wallet. He slid his license out and held it up for her to see.

She leaned in, pretending to scrutinize it as if she didn't trust him, which was a lie. She did. She probably shouldn't, but she was a rather trusting person in general.

"And as for knowing where you live, you also shouldn't let a man you've just met walk you home. It's entirely unsafe. However, you're out of options right now, and I could easily look at your lease at any time and find your address if I wanted."

True. Defeated on this issue, she led him to the front of the store, let them out, then locked the door.

He checked it to make sure it was secure. "By the way, don't ever leave it unlocked like you did tonight. Not while you're here alone at night."

"Yes, Daddy," she drawled before she could stop herself yet again.

He chuckled and lifted her chin, meeting her wide eyes with his gaze. "Watch it, Little one. I think I like the sound of that."

She inhaled sharply and took a step back. "I should get home."

"That's the plan." He followed her as soon as she started walking, keeping a hand on the small of her back the entire time. He also ensured that she walked on the inside of the side-walk closest to the buildings, and he grabbed her waist when they came to a street before letting her step off the sidewalk.

She almost giggled when he looked both ways, seeming to silently admonish her. There wasn't a single car out, not coming from any direction.

She was relieved when they reached her condo because the sexual tension and energy running between them was almost her undoing.

The overprotective, dominant, alpha Daddy man even took

her keys out of her hand, opened her door, and stepped into her apartment to look around before handing her back her keyring. "Thanks for indulging me. I'll sleep better knowing you made it home safely."

"You're welcome." She slid past him, entering as he stepped out.

"Lock the door behind me, Ellie. I mean it."

"Yes, Sir," she murmured. Somehow, the honorific no longer sounded misplaced. Maybe this man was a Daddy, or at least a Dom.

Chapter Two

It took Garrett a few hours of tossing and turning during the night before he was positive where he'd seen Ellie before. Blaze. Definitely. And it wasn't a coincidence that she'd copped such an attitude with him, dressed like a young girl, or sung a childish song she'd made up at the top of her lungs.

Ellie was a Little. He was sure of it. And he intended to prove it.

The next two days were torture while he waited for Friday night, hoping she would go to Blaze and he could catch her there. He hadn't been to the club for several months. He'd been busy. He'd also been a bit disenchanted after ending things with his previous girlfriend.

Meredith had been a model submissive, and the two of them had dated for six months. But she wasn't a Little, and in the end, he knew he was kidding himself if he thought he could give up his inclination toward being a Daddy permanently.

The two of them had gone their separate ways amicably, but Garrett hadn't had the desire to return to the club scene and start looking for a new submissive yet.

Until now. Until Ellie. The woman was a whirlwind of fire, energy, and spunk. If he wasn't mistaken, she had a pretty strong Little side, a bit of a bratty edge, and a sassy mouth that would frequently land her over a Daddy's lap with a palm to her bottom.

Garrett was hoping he might get the chance to be that Daddy. He'd even gone so far as to flat-out ask her if she'd had a husband or a boyfriend, and he'd seen no evidence of either when he'd dropped her off. At least he seemed to have jumped that hurdle.

Ellie hadn't been overly receptive to the idea of starting something with him, and that made him nervous. But perhaps she'd simply been caught off guard. He hoped if he "bumped into her" in a safe location like Blaze, she might be inclined to give him a chance.

Work had kept him later than he'd wanted, so by the time he arrived at the club, he was frazzled. He needed to unwind. He needed to set his gaze on Ellie.

He had no guarantee whatsoever that she was even a member. Even if she had been at some point and he was right—that he had indeed seen her at the club—that didn't mean she would be there tonight.

The moment he stepped out of the main room and entered the hallway, he saw her. She was sitting in the daycare with two other Littles he recognized—Daisy, who owned the florist boutique on the same strip as Ellie's cupcake shop, and Riley, who bartended at Blaze two nights a week. They were coloring. Ellie took his breath away and caused him to freeze in his spot.

Damn. She was more than what he'd seen the other night at her shop. So much more. She had on short pink overalls over a tight white tank top, matching pink knee socks, and white tennis shoes. Her hair was in pigtails high on her head. He knew her hair was about shoulder length, so the pigtails were little balls of hair that looked more like puppy ears.

He jerked his gaze to the side when he noticed one of the dungeon masters approaching.

"Hey, Garrett. How's it going? I haven't seen you in a while."

Garrett held out a hand. "I've been good." He'd known Tarson Kirkwood for a long time. The man was a gem and an amazing Daddy when he wasn't working at Blaze. He went by Bear in the club. He liked to think he was a giant grizzly bear, gruff and no nonsense, but Garrett knew the Littles giggled and called him Teddy behind his back.

Bear nodded toward the daycare. "Got your eye on anyone in particular?"

"Yep." Garrett turned his attention back to the adorable Little who was intently coloring.

Bear chuckled. "Ellie?"

"Yep."

"You've picked a sweet one. I'll leave you to it."

"Thanks, Bear."

The dungeon master wandered off, leaving Garrett contemplating the Little he hoped to woo.

For a long time, he simply watched her.

He must have stared at her long and hard enough for the hairs on the back of her neck to stand up, because suddenly she turned around and caught his gaze.

Her eyes went wide in that adorable way he'd seen more than once the other night, and she blinked several times before finally pushing away from the table. She said something to her companions he couldn't hear before making her way toward him.

"Uh... What are you doing here, Mr. Erickson?" She rubbed her palms together.

"I knew I'd seen you somewhere before. I was right."

She looked down and dragged the toe of one white sneaker back and forth on the floor. Fucking adorable.

He needed to take his time. Say the right things. Handle her carefully. She had every right to be very nervous. Being discovered by someone outside the club was nerve-wracking under any circumstances. Being found by the owner of your building had to be stressful.

He leaned one shoulder against the wall at his side, forcing himself to keep his hands to himself for now. "Please don't panic. I would never tell a soul about seeing you at Blaze. Rule number one in the fetish community."

She lifted her face and licked her sweet lips. They were as full and pink as they'd been the other night. He hadn't imagined that part. Hell, he hadn't imagined any part. Her eyes were a deep brown that sucked him in. Her skin was soft and golden, but not dark enough to hide her rosy cheeks.

"Can we go somewhere and talk?" he asked, trying to control his voice so he didn't sound as desperate as he felt.

"You mean like here at the club? Or somewhere else?" she asked tentatively.

"Whatever makes you the most comfortable, Ellie."

"What exactly do you want to talk about?" She licked her lips again.

He wanted to kiss those lips. He hoped to God there would come a day when he would be permitted to. "Whatever you want to talk about. Anything. Everything. I like you. I'd like to get to know you."

"Don't you think that's kind of inappropriate with you owning the building I'm renting and all?" she hedged. There wasn't a lot of umph behind her words, though.

"I don't see a problem. It's not like I'm your boss. I just own the building." He shrugged. "No big deal."

She fidgeted, threading her fingers together and shifting her weight back and forth. "I mean, what if we started something and then it went bad and then you took it out on me and raised my rent or found some way to get me to break my lease? I love that location and the space. I don't want to risk my business."

Garrett fought the urge to chuckle, knowing she was dead serious even though her rambling thoughts were slightly outlandish. It made her even cuter. "So, you've thought about it then, haven't you?"

"Thought about what, Sir?"

God, he loved it when she called him Sir. It made his dick flinch inside his black jeans. "Starting something with me. I mean, you've put so much thought into it since we met that you've come up with the wildest, worst-case scenario known to man as an excuse."

Her cheeks pinkened further. Again, adorably. After chewing on the corner of her bottom lip for a moment, she released it and sighed. "Maybe."

Now he did chuckle. He also reached out to cup her cheek, stroking her skin with his thumb. "I promise not to get revenge in any way on you if things don't work out. I'm not that kind of asshole. I'm a nice guy." He bent his knees a bit to make them more eye-to-eye. "A Daddy, Ellie."

She inhaled slowly. "I guess I didn't do anything to hide my Little the other night, did I?"

"Not really. No."

"I wasn't expecting anyone to come into the shop while I was in my Little head space. You caught me off guard."

"And I'm glad I did. Your door was unlocked. I wasn't kidding about that, Little one. If you were mine and I found you acting that reckless, I would take you over my knee and spank your bottom so hard you wouldn't be able to sit comfortably the next day." He lifted a brow to make sure she fully understood.

She shuddered. "I won't do it again, Sir."

"See that you don't. Now, what about my suggestion? Can we go sit somewhere slightly more private and talk?"

"I guess." She glanced over her shoulder toward the adult age-play daycare area longingly.

He slid his hand down to hers, taking it gently. "Come on. I promise not to keep you all night. I'll bring you back to finish coloring your picture in a while."

"Okay."

Garrett felt like he'd jumped another high hurdle as he led Ellie to one of the lounge rooms. Instead of choosing a loveseat or couch, he took a chance and aimed straight for an armchair.

After sitting, he drew her between his legs and lifted her onto one knee.

She squirmed and started to get off. "I'm too big for your lap, Sir."

"Don't be silly. You're just right." He anchored her with an arm around her waist.

"Sir..." she complained. "I'm going to hurt your leg."

He frowned. "Please don't tell me you think you're too large for my lap. That's nonsense."

"I'm not exactly small, Sir."

"Thank God. If I was interested in a skinny Little girl with a bony butt, I would have found one. But I like my Little girls to have curves and enough flesh on their bottoms that I won't feel like I'm hurting them when I swat their naughty butts."

She slouched a bit, seemingly resigned to remaining where he wanted her. Hurdle number three.

"I love this outfit, by the way," he said to change the subject. "You look so pretty in this color of pink." He tapped her nose.

She finally smiled. "Thank you, Sir."

"Is pink your favorite color?"

She shrugged. "Sometimes. I like all colors."

"Is that why you were making rainbow sprinkle cupcakes the other night?"

She grinned wider and nodded.

"Tell me more about yourself. How old are you?"

"Thirty."

"How long have you lived in the area?"

"A few months."

"Where were you before that?"

"I was living outside of town with my grandmother. After I

graduated from college, her health started failing, so I moved in with her to help take care of her."

"Wow. That was a huge responsibility. Where is she now?" he asked, knowing the probable answer.

"She died six months ago."

"I'm so sorry, Little one. It sounds like you were very close."

"Yes. She was my only family. She raised me from the time I was five. She wanted me to put her in a home, but there was no way I could do that. I stayed with her to the very end."

"Fulltime? Did you have a job?"

She shook her head, her pigtails shaking, making her look younger. "Not while she was still alive. After she died, I started working as a pastry chef in a hotel. It turned out my grandmother had a sizable inheritance from my grandfather. He passed before I was born, but his family was wealthy. My grandmother lived rather frugally, but she left me plenty of money."

"Enough to open a bakery now that she's gone," he mused.

"Exactly. It was what she wanted me to do. She knew my dream was to own a cupcake shop, so she insisted I do so as soon as she was gone. I won't let her down. I'm going to have the best cupcake shop in the state," she insisted emphatically.

"I have no doubt." He grinned as he tapped her nose again. "And the prettiest!"

"Yes!" she agreed, unconsciously wiggling slightly to nestle herself against his supporting arm.

Garrett commanded his body not to respond to the delightful woman on his lap. He didn't want to scare her away. Fighting his usual ironclad control, his body reacted to the curvy enchantress.

Ellie tilted her head to the side to look at him closely. "I can't get involved with a stranger. Tell me about yourself."

"My name is Garrett Erickson. I'm thirty-eight years old. I used to be a professional football player but had to make a life change when I was injured. Now, I own commercial real estate and watch sports on TV."

"Do you miss it?" she asked with small lines crinkling her forehead.

"I do and I don't. With everything, there are positives and negatives. I have more free time now to visit Blaze and search for my Little."

"Are you really a Daddy? I mean... Some Doms find Littles cute at first but don't want to deal with our quirks."

"You mean like skipping bedtime and making cupcakes at two in the morning?" he asked, the corners of his mouth curving up in delight.

Ellie shrugged and studied him for a few moments. "I've never had a Daddy. You know—a real one."

"Have you had trouble with a pretender?" Garrett felt his protective urges spring to life. To his own surprise, he was ready to confront anyone who had messed with Ellie.

"Nothing bad," she rushed to assure him.

"How did you know he wasn't a Daddy?" Garrett probed.

"It was a feeling inside. I can't really explain it, but I just knew." She raised her hand to twirl her fingers through one pigtail as her big brown eyes seemed to lose focus.

"You called me Daddy within five minutes of meeting me," Garrett reminded her softly. To his delight, Ellie nodded immediately. Then, her face flooded with color.

"I felt it, too," he reassured her softly.

"Really?"

"Really."

They sat there quietly for several long seconds. When she started to wiggle, Garrett asked, "How long have you been coming to Blaze?"

"I found Blaze a few months ago. Hanging out with the Littles is fun."

"What do you think of the rest of the club?"

"Oh, I don't go there," she rushed to tell him. "I feel comfortable in the daycare, but I'm scared to explore everywhere else."

He rubbed her back to reassure Ellie. *What is it about this Little girl?* "Maybe you'd like to tour with me some day?"

Ellie shrugged her shoulders and wrinkled her nose. "Maybe."

She twirled her pigtail again before changing the subject. "Would you like to go color?"

"I can't think of anything I'd rather do."

She scooted off his lap with a grin and took his hand. Tugging him back into her safe place, Ellie sat down at her spot and patted the chair next to her. After he sat down, she introduced him to the other Littles.

"This is Garrett. He's a Daddy. He's going to color with us, okay?"

Chapter Three

Stepping into Little Cakes the next morning, Ellie left the door unlocked. The delivery truck would be there any time with her tables and chairs. Walking through the swinging door that separated the kitchen from the bakery display shelves, she set her screwdriver and cellphone on the top of the industrial refrigerator where she wouldn't lose them before stepping back to open the protective folder she carried.

Garrett's picture looked up at her. "It's just perfect. I thought it would be a joke to pick a unicorn for him to color," she announced to the empty kitchen. Shifting around the recipes fixed with magnets on the front of the refrigerator, Ellie attached Garrett's colorful artwork on the stainless-steel surface.

She stepped back to look at it. He hadn't gone out of the lines once! The unicorn stood proudly in the center of the page displaying his multicolored mane and tail. His body was silver with black shoes. Ellie traced his name at the bottom. She'd made him sign it, of course.

A noise out front drew her attention away from the artwork. Ellie grabbed her screwdriver and whirled around to march back to the front of the shop. Expecting to see a man looking official with a clipboard, she stopped in her tracks to see four rough-looking men pawing through the few things scattered through the sales area.

"Hey! Are you the delivery guys?" Ellie asked, nervously. She forced herself to stand up straight as if their presence didn't spook her.

The four men looked at each other and grinned. One stepped toward her. Ellie backed up a few paces. Why hadn't she grabbed her phone?

"No, we're more the pick-up type of crew. This is a cupcake store, huh? We'd be willing to take some off your hands," a grubby man with shifting eyes suggested.

"Sorry, I'm not open yet. Just getting set up. You'll have to come back another day," Ellie suggested as her mind raced, trying to figure out a way to handle this situation.

The store was in a perfectly safe location. She'd never seen anything sketchy happening as she'd worked in the store late at night or during the day. What was she going to do if they threatened her? Gripping the screwdriver tightly in her hand, Ellie was determined to protect her new business.

When the obvious leader of the pack took another step toward her, Ellie bristled. She wasn't going to let anyone take this dream from her. "Look, I don't know who you are and I don't care. The store isn't open and you'll have to leave."

"Isn't that cute, Ben? She wants us to leave," one of the other three joked, talking to the guy in charge.

"Yes. You need to go now." Ellie tried to control the warble of fright from her voice and failed.

"Just what are you going to do if we refuse?" Ben asked.

Bang! Bang! Bang!

Ellie whirled to see Garrett's muscular form filling the doorway as he struck the metal frame.

As the unwelcome visitors turned, Garrett took several photos of their surprised faces before addressing them, "You have been asked to leave the store. I'm telling you as the property owner that you need to move on. I now have your photos and will share them with my contacts at the police station."

"They can't pick us up for anything. The door was open. We just came in to see if anything was for sale," Ben argued as he backed toward the other men.

Garrett walked to Ellie's side. "You picked the wrong place to visit. Nothing will happen to this woman or her business. Do you understand?"

With nods, the men slinked through the open door. Ellie turned and threw herself against Garrett's broad chest. "Thank you for coming!"

"You are in so much trouble, Rainbow," Garrett lectured.

"Hey! I've got a delivery for Little Cakes. Are you Ellie Willmoth?" A man called from the door.

Ellie sprang away from Garrett to see a man dressed in a blue uniform with a tablet in his hand in her doorway. "Yes! I'm Ellie."

"Sign here, ma'am, and we'll start bringing in the boxes."

"Of course." Ellie walked quickly toward him to sign her name with the stylus he offered. She watched the man prop open the door with a rubber wedge from his pocket before returning to the large truck parked at the curb out front. A shaky breath escaped her lungs as she tried to dispel the scare.

"You've earned your first punishment, Ellie."

"What? You can't punish me," she argued.

The return of the delivery guys pushing two dollies filled with large boxes interrupted his answer. Ellie gestured with the screwdriver toward an empty corner of the store. When they dropped off the first round of boxes, she ran over eagerly to open the top of one box, using the screwdriver to punch through the tape. Peering inside, she saw a bunch of parts filling the cardboard container.

"I don't suppose you paid for these to be assembled?" Garrett asked from behind her.

"I thought they'd come out of the box with maybe just the

screws to hold the top on the tables. This looks a bit more involved," she observed.

Garrett held his hand out for the screwdriver she still held tightly.

"You don't have to help," she assured him quickly. "I can do it."

"I have this morning free. Some of those parts look heavy. Besides, we need to talk after they leave."

Ellie nodded, accepting her fate. She knew she'd messed up. "Those guys scared me," she admitted.

"They frightened me, too."

"You were scared?" she gasped.

"I don't want you to be hurt. There are bad people in the world. Hopefully, I got through to those men and they won't come back. I'll hire a security force to patrol for a few weeks."

When she opened her mouth to protest, he held a hand up to stop her. "Not only to take care of you, but the other tenants as well."

That did make her feel better to think someone would watch over the whole strip center. Ellie watched Garrett settle on the floor with her screwdriver and a set of instructions. He joked with the delivery people as they continued to bring in boxes of tables and chairs. By the time the men had unloaded her order, Garrett already had two tables put together.

He stood as the men brought in the last load. "Count the boxes, Ellie. Let's make sure you have everything."

She counted the boxes of tabletops and chairs to compare to her order. *Huh, that's not right.*

"What are you missing?" Garrett asked.

"I think there's a box of chairs missing," she told him, shuffling through her papers. "I'm sure I've miscounted."

"How many should you have, Ellie?"

"There should be twelve boxes of four chairs and ten tables," she answered distractedly as she counted again.

Garrett held his hand out for her pen. Walking through the

sea of boxes, he labeled each one with a capital T or C and a number. Soon, everything was counted. There were only eleven boxes of chairs.

"Guys, could you check on the truck to see if there's one more box? We're missing a set of chairs."

"Hold on." One guy jogged to the open truck bay. He disappeared from view but they could hear boxes being scooted around as he checked.

"Yeah, it's here!" he called.

Within minutes, they'd offloaded the last box. Ellie signed for the delivery. With an efficacy attesting to lots of practice, they grabbed the door stop, closed the back of the truck, and jumped into the cab. Within a few minutes, they were headed to their next stop, leaving Ellie alone with Garrett.

"You don't have to stay and help me. I know you're busy," Ellie said quickly.

"Little girl, lock the door," Garrett directed with a stern look.

"It's daylight. Nothing will happen now," she protested.

"Lock the door."

Click! Ellie turned back to Garrett and demanded, "Are you happy now?"

"No. Kitchen, now."

"I'm not baking today. My schedule says *put tables together*," she corrected him, pulling up her calendar and displaying her task for the day.

"You do not wish to receive your punishment for endangering yourself in front of the windows, do you?" Garrett asked quietly.

"I don't wish to be punished. Period," she sassed back, knowing already that she was making a big mistake.

"You were warned." Garrett stalked forward. Moving too fast for her to react, he leaned over and scooped her up over his shoulder. He turned so her bottom faced squarely to the large windows lining the store front.

"What? No! Let me down!" Ellie demanded, trying to free herself by flailing around.

Whack! Garrett's immense hand landed on her plump bottom.

Ellie shrieked with anger at being controlled and the jolt of pain. "Stop this! Put me down!"

Whack! He seemed to completely ignore her orders as he easily contained her movements. "Oh, look! There's the mailman. Would you like to wave hello?" Garrett asked, his breathing even and unstressed. He rotated to let Ellie look through the glass.

The postal worker was actually walking down the sidewalk toward Little Cakes! He stopped at each store front and dropped envelopes and small packages through the mail slot next to the door. Ellie froze as the mailman tugged the next set of mail from his satchel. He was on the other side of the curved strip center and could look up at any time to see her slung over Garrett's shoulder.

"Kitchen! I'll go in the kitchen!" she conceded.

Garrett carried her through the swinging door and set Ellie on her feet by the large worktable. "Lean over the table, Little girl," he instructed.

"What are you going to do?"

"Finish your spanking."

"I don't really need to be punished. I'm sure I was perfectly safe," she assured him.

"How scared were you before I walked in?" he asked quietly.

Ellie stared at him. She'd been on the edge of terrified. Not really there, but definitely on the border of being petrified. *I'm not going to tell him that!*

"Maybe twenty-five percent scared," she lied.

"You've just added five more swats for not telling the truth."

Studying his face, she knew nothing she said would sway him. "I'm sorry?" she tried, hoping to mollify him.

"Locking the door when you're here by yourself will help keep you safe. I was more than fifty percent scared when I walked in and found you with those men. What if I hadn't been here?"

The possible consequences flooded her mind. There was no way she could have fought all four of those guys. She could have screamed for help but would anyone have heard her? "It was stupid. I'm sorry."

Garrett stepped forward and wrapped an arm around her, pulling her close. "I don't know how you've weaved yourself into my life, Ellie, but you're important to me. Daddies know when they meet their Littles."

"You think I'm yours?" she asked, staring up at him.

"Yes. You're mine." Garrett pulled her flush against his body. Leaning over, he kissed Ellie softly.

She rose onto her tiptoes to meet his touch. Opening her mouth as his tongue swept between her lips, Ellie gripped his shirt to hold on as he explored the inside of her mouth. He tasted like mint toothpaste with an underlying spice that was Garrett's alone. Ellie never wanted the kiss to end.

"Oh!" she protested when he lifted his head.

"I know, Rainbow. I want to kiss you more as well." He chuckled when she pursed her lips, inviting more. "More after your punishment."

"Can't we just forget that? I'll remember to lock the door," she promised.

"Over the table, Rainbow."

His tone was unyielding. She wasn't going to get out of this. Allowing him to spank her would mean that Ellie agreed to his claim of being her Daddy. Studying his face, she saw concern and caring underlying the strict expression. The picture pinned on the refrigerator door caught her attention. Garrett had been nice to all the other Littles coloring, but she had been the center of his attention. The flirting from her friends Daisy and Riley had died out as they realized he was only interested in her. She'd known then that he truly wanted to be her Daddy.

Ellie nodded, acknowledging the silent question that lingered between them. Slowly, she turned around, giving him all the time in the world to stop her. "Do you really have to spank me?" She appealed her fate, peeking over her shoulder.

"Now, Ellie."

When she collapsed to the table, his hand pressed her against the cold steel surface. "I will not allow you to endanger yourself. Daddies take care of Littles," he lectured.

Garrett's free hand swatted her displayed curves. Ellie wiggled, trying to get away. She inhaled deeply to yell when she heard a rustle and a thud come from the front of the store.

"Your mail's here," Garrett announced before spanking her again.

Ellie shoved her hands over her mouth. She didn't want anyone to know he was spanking her. The next few swats landed, and her entire bottom felt like it was on fire. Tears gathered in her eyes and rolled down her cheeks to puddle on the table. Ellie crossed her arms on the hard surface and buried her face against them to hide.

"Let Daddy see your pretty face," Garrett directed when she turned to look down at the table.

She shook her head, not wanting him to see her cry.

"I need to see your face, Rainbow. I can't tell if your punishment is harming you without seeing your eyes."

His voice was low and commanding. She couldn't resist his directions. She pressed her cheek against the countertop, allowing him to see her tears. Ellie knew her face was blotchy and ugly. Some people could cry and look adorable. Ellie looked wretched.

"Thank you, Little girl. The last five and then I'll hold you," he shared.

"Please," Ellie whispered.

The last five swats landed in quick succession. She didn't

even have time to gasp between them as he peppered her bottom. Blinded by the tears that flowed freely from her eyes, Ellie went limp on the table, relinquishing her control completely to him.

Garrett's hand smoothed over her bottom, easing the sting slightly as he leaned over her. "You did very well, Rainbow. Let me hold you now," he whispered intimately against her ear as he scooped her body from the worktable.

Held close to his heart, Ellie wrapped her arms around his muscular torso and lifted her lips for her reward. His mouth crashed down on hers in a demanding kiss that asked everything from her. Garrett's hand stroked down her body to grip her punished bottom and press her to his hard shaft. She squeezed her thighs together, feeling the intimate wetness her punishment had created. Their attraction was undeniable.

Daddy!

Chapter Four

Setting down the cold bottle of water, Ellie looked up at Garrett from her perch on top of the work table. He had taken perfect care of her as she recovered from her spanking. After getting her water and a cupcake with sprinkles from the refrigerator, he'd wrapped his arm around her waist.

"You don't have to stay with me," she told him.

"Yes, I do. You've got tables and chairs to put together."

"I can do it. I know you have to be busy."

"You just skyrocketed to the top of my importance list. How are you feeling?" he asked, brushing her hair back from her face.

"My butt hurts."

Laughing, he bopped her nose affectionately. "Good, Rainbow. You need a reminder to take care of yourself. What's the lesson you've learned today?"

"Know when you're coming and lock the door?" she suggested with a twinge of sass.

"Just a warning, Little one. Next time, your pants and panties will be around your ankles."

Ellie swallowed hard and met his gaze. Those beautiful

green eyes seemed to see past the persona she shared with the rest of the world. Garrett knew who she was. "Yes, Daddy."

"Now, let's have some music and get all that furniture together," he suggested, lifting her off the table.

Within minutes, Ellie had her favorite station playing loud enough that she could hear it even when upside down in a box, pulling the parts out.

Garrett was the perfect companion. His deep bass voice sang along with hers as Ellie danced her way around the furniture he created. She arranged and rearranged the tables and chairs until they were in the perfect spots. Garrett never made fun of her. He just shifted over if he was in the way.

"Yikes!" Ellie yipped after she flounced into a chair at the last table. She jumped to her feet and whirled to glare at Garrett when he chuckled. "It's not funny!"

"Are you going to remember to lock the door when you're alone?" he asked.

"Yes."

"Good girl." Before she could protest anymore, Garrett looked at his watch. "I need to check in with my office. What are you going to do this afternoon?"

"I have a new cupcake to test."

"What flavor this time?" he asked.

"It's a surprise."

"Hmm! I guess you're allowed to have creative secrets." Garrett winked at her, sending a delighted shiver through Ellie. She loved that he had a funny side as well as a stern Daddy personality.

"May I pick you up this evening to return to Blaze?" Garrett asked, stalking forward to wrap his arms around her.

"I'd like that." Ellie smiled at him before suggesting, "Nine o'clock?"

"Perfect, Rainbow." He leaned forward to kiss her deeply. Garrett stepped back with a reluctant shake of his head. Taking her hand, he led her to the door. "Lock up after me. Until I have some closure on what those men were doing, I want you to be very careful."

"Yes, Sir!" Ellie saluted saucily with her free hand and then bolted forward when his hand lightly swatted her bottom, reminding her to behave. "Oops!"

"Oops, indeed. I'll see you at nine."

She stood at the plate glass window and watched him cross the parking lot to a large SUV. It suited him. Garrett was subtle elegance to the core. He didn't need an expensive sports car to make him look good. Those battered jeans hugged him in all the right places. Ellie waved when he turned and caught her watching.

"Time to get to work," she ordered herself. After double-checking the lock, she grabbed her phone and cranked up the volume. It was baking time!

Her latest batch was cooling when her phone started dancing across the table. Ellie grabbed it before the device tumbled to the ground. Trying not to smear the florescent blue icing she was perfecting over the keys, Ellie answered, "Hello? Oh, wait a minute. Let me turn down the music, I can't hear you."

"Little girl, I'm at your house. Did you lose track of time?" Garrett's dry voice sounded in her ear.

"Crap! It can't be nine!" Ellie pulled the phone from her ear to check the time. 8:57 pm.

"I can be there in five minutes. Maybe fifteen." She shook her head, looking at the kitchen. There was no way she'd make it out of there in less than an hour.

"Are you tired, Little girl?" his voice asked softly, making her aware of the ache at the small of her back and legs.

"Exhausted," she confessed, leaning against the table as the adrenaline that had kept her going evaporated.

"Clean up what you need to, I'm on my way to get you. I'll

order a pizza and pick it up first. You need more to eat than cupcakes and frosting."

"Thanks, Garrett. I'll watch for you," she promised.

After scooping frosting into plastic storage containers for tomorrow, Ellie ran all the dirty dishes through the industrial washer and left them on the racks to air dry. She'd just swept and mopped when a faint beep sounded from the front of the store. Hanging her apron on the corner of a rack, Ellie headed into the front room with her phone and keys.

"Let me," Garrett suggested, taking the keys from her fingers and locking the door securely behind her. "Come on, Rainbow. Inside." He helped her climb into the tall SUV and leaned in to kiss her lightly before pulling the belt over her lap.

"Sorry," she whispered.

"You don't need to be sorry. I know you're trying to get ready for the grand opening. I won't, however, let you run yourself into the ground. You'll need your energy to run Little Cakes every day." When she nodded, he closed the door and rounded the hood to slide in next to her.

"The pizza smells amazing. I hope you ordered a large."

"The biggest they have plus extra cheese," he assured her.

"I have some people coming to apply for a job tomorrow," she shared as he started the vehicle.

"Good. You'll need reliable staff. Let me know if you need me to run any background checks for you."

"Thanks." Ellie leaned back against the seat and closed her eyes. She'd just rest while they were driving. Within moments, she'd crashed into sleep.

A loud snore made Garrett laugh quietly. Ellie embraced everything with the same vigor she did her cooking. Instead of taking Ellie home, he headed to his house. Ellie could spend the night with him.

A few minutes from his driveway, she quieted and sniffed. Rubbing her eyes, Ellie murmured, "Where are we?" She looked around, trying to orient herself.

"We're almost to my house. I thought you could eat and then I'll tuck you into my nursery."

"You have a nursery?" she asked, turning in the seat to face him.

"I do. Would you like to see it?"

"Yes. I'm not ready to sleep with you yet, Garrett," Ellie blurted.

"Okay. Nursery time until you're ready to sleep in your Daddy's big bed," he agreed readily as he turned onto his driveway. The lights came on automatically inside as the garage door rose. Garrett appreciated the welcoming feel of his home now more than ever.

"It's so pretty," Ellie complimented.

"Let me show you around," he suggested. "Stay there. Daddy will let you out, Rainbow."

She nodded and relaxed against the seat back. Garrett watched her as he grabbed the pizza from the back. He set the box on the roof as he opened her door and leaned in to unlatch her seatbelt. "I'll take you home anytime you wish, Little girl."

"Thanks," she whispered.

"Let's go eat some pizza." After helping her out, Garrett snagged the large container and took Ellie's hand to tug her into the house. "Sit at the counter, Rainbow."

He grabbed two plates and opened the box to place a piece on each of their plates. Immediately, Ellie picked up her slice and took a huge bite. She froze in place when she wiggled on the padded seat.

"Careful," he warned. Garrett filled two glasses with ice and water before snapping a lid on one to place in front of her.

"This is amazing!" Ellie complimented, taking another huge bite.

"Small bites, Little girl. Don't choke," Garrett warned as he lifted his slice to his mouth. "Mmm, it is good."

She grinned at him.

"Feel better after your nap?"

"I didn't snore, did I? My grandmother always said I did, but I think she exaggerated," Ellie shared as she chewed.

"She told the truth."

"Really? I snored?" Ellie took another bite and chewed thoughtfully before double-checking, "Like a cute snore, right? Not like a roaring chainsaw?"

"The leather is still attached to my passenger seat," Garrett reassured her.

"Oh, good. Wait! What does that mean?" she asked, tilting her head sideways to look at him quizzically.

"Let's just leave it at you snore," he suggested.

"Oh, heavenly sprinkles! I snore that bad?"

"Yep!" he confirmed, taking another bite to hide his grin. Garrett absolutely loved the pink tinge that colored her skin. *Adorable!*

"I'll never be able to look at you again," she dramatically despaired, taking another bite and chewing.

"You don't know how loud *I* snore. Maybe I'm even louder than you are," Garrett proposed.

"That would be awesome. Then, I wouldn't be self-conscious."

He stroked his hand through her hair, smoothing the locks ruffled by her nap. "You don't need to be worried. I still brought you home."

"That's right! You did!" she cheered up.

After taking a drink, she asked, "Did you really mean it when you said you have a nursery—a Little's nursery?"

"Yes."

"Can I see it?" she asked, sliding off her stool.

"After you finish that piece of pizza. I want something in your tummy before we brush your teeth and put you to bed."

"Okay," she agreed, good-naturedly. Climbing back onto the padded seat, she munched the crunchy crust.

He loved watching her nibble.

"Don't rush. I'm not in any hurry," Ellie told him, pushing her plate away to pillow her head on her arm.

Garrett popped the last of his piece into his mouth and stood. Ushering her before him, he led her to the guest bathroom. "Go in and potty. There are fresh toothbrushes and toothpaste in the drawer. Jump into the shower and rinse the sugar from your skin. You're sticky, Little girl."

He groaned as she licked the inside of her forearm to test his theory. "I'll get you a T-shirt to wear in your crib."

Yawning, she nodded. Garrett watched her turn and walk sleepily into the bathroom. He'd step in to help if she was too exhausted to take care of herself. Right now, he didn't want to scare her by moving too fast. After the toilet flushed and he heard the crinkle of a wrapper, he jogged to his room to snag something for her to wear.

To his delight, she sang endearingly off-tune in the shower. He eased the door open and set the shirt on a dry spot before resuming his wait in the hall. In a few minutes, she appeared in the doorway. Swallowing the possessive surge that brewed inside him at the sight of her dressed in his clothing, Garrett wrapped an arm around her to guide her into the nursery. She was the first Little to ever step inside.

Garrett watched her blink as she looked around. "Playtime later, Rainbow. Time to be in your crib." He lifted her into the elevated bed and settled her under the covers.

Ellie wiggled a few times but settled into place when he patted her back. With a soft sigh, she closed her eyes and drifted into sleep. Her adorably loud snore clued him in that she was out for the night.

Chapter Five

Rubbing her eyes, Ellie sat up in the beautiful crib. She stroked the curving slats on the sides before looking around. It was a Little girl's paradise with a huge bin of toys and games on one side and a big picture window with a cushioned seat on the other. Books lined the nearby shelf, beckoning her to select one and curl up to read.

Ellie peeked over the side to the carpet below. "That's a long way down," she whispered to herself. Rolling onto her tummy, she wiggled her legs over the edge and dropped slowly to her feet.

Feeling proud of her gymnastics, Ellie decided to go surprise her Daddy. That thought startled her—not that she'd sneak up on Garrett, but that she already considered him to be her Daddy. She needed to see him now.

It wasn't hard to find Garrett. The enormous master bedroom was right across the hall. She tiptoed in, memorizing the sight of his massive form sprawled over the covers. Only one section of the sheet covered part of his muscular butt. The rest of his body lay exposed to her view.

Lecturing herself to stop staring, Ellie crept around the bed to see his face. The view from all angles was as spectacular as the first. *Wait! He's not snoring!* she thought indignantly.

Climbing up on the bed, she stared down at him. When those green eyes blinked open to meet her gaze, she informed him, "Daddies aren't supposed to lie."

Garrett gave her a slow sexy smile and then reached out and snagged her around the waist, hauling her against his side as he rolled to face her. "How did I lie?" he asked as he bopped her on the nose with one finger.

She squirmed against him, giggling. "You told me you snored."

He grinned. "Ah. And I wasn't snoring just now?"

"Nope." It was hard to concentrate on what he was saying with his huge, hard, naked body pressed against her. The only thing between them was his T-shirt she was wearing.

"Maybe you caught me at a good moment. I probably don't snore constantly." He lifted a brow.

"Mmm." She worried her bottom lip with her teeth. "Maybe." She narrowed her gaze at him until she could only barely see him through tiny slits, and then she shook a finger in front of him. "You should probably fess up now because eventually I will find out the truth, and then your punishment will be more severe than if you'd told the truth in the first place. You've dug a huge hole now, mister."

He chuckled, the vibrations making her nipples stiffen as he grabbed her much smaller hand and brought it to his lips to kiss her knuckles. "I'm afraid it doesn't work that way, Little girl."

She pouted dramatically, pushing her lip out. "That's no fair."

"Life's not fair." His gaze changed to something more serious as he stared down at her, still gripping her fingers.

Her heart hammered in her chest and she squeezed her thighs together as wetness pooled between her legs. It was hard to keep from wiggling with his warmth surrounding her.

46

"Daddy makes the rules, Little girl. Not you. Your job is to follow the rules."

She hmphed. "Fine."

"Want to change your tone, Little girl?" His brow rose.

"Sorry, Daddy."

"That's better. Now, how did you get down from your crib without help?"

"It was up very high, Daddy. I had to slide off the edge carefully until I jumped the last part to the floor."

"Do you think that was safe?"

She swallowed, but his tone made her squirm even more. She'd never had a Daddy like this. A real one. She'd never slept at a Daddy's house either. Every minute she spent with Garrett was magical. Could it be real? Could he be her forever Daddy? "No, Sir," she whispered.

"I won't punish you this morning because we didn't discuss the nursery rules yet, but from now on, when you sleep in your crib, I'll put the side up, and you'll wait for Daddy to come get you. Understood?"

"Yes, Daddy."

Ellie dropped her gaze away from his to gather her courage. "Um... Do I always have to sleep in my crib?"

He tilted her chin back up to look in her eyes. "It's important for a Little girl to get adjusted to a new schedule. When you can sleep soundly in your crib, then sometimes you can choose to sleep in Daddy's bed. Would you like that?"

She nodded and felt her cheeks warm. Before she could focus on her embarrassment, he asked, "Now. I have a question."

She widened her eyes. "What?"

"You sure are squirmy this morning. Is that because you're aroused?"

Heat rushed over her cheeks and she glanced away. "Maybe..."

He released her hand to slide his down over her hip and

around to the back of her thigh. "If I reach between your legs, will I find you wet, Little girl?"

She whimpered as his fingers slowly eased higher. "Well... It's your fault. You were lying here naked, and..."

He grinned. "And what?" His fingers inched closer to her core.

Her breath hitched as he reached so close she almost begged him to touch her.

"And what, Rainbow?" he prompted again.

She blinked, trying to remember the question while he hovered so very close to exactly where she wanted him to touch her. *Oh right.* "You must know how sexy you are, Daddy. Don't be silly. Even part of your butt cheek was exposed."

"So you were watching me sleep, huh?" His eyes danced with humor.

"Maybe... Just for a minute. Long enough to know you don't snore," she reminded him.

He chuckled. "Long enough for your pussy to get wet, huh?" He gripped the back of her thigh and hitched her top leg up over his hip.

She gasped as her legs were parted, exposing her sex to the cool air. She was really, really wet, and he was about to find out. She reached for his shoulder and gripped with her fingertips. "Daddy..."

His hand slid back around her thigh. "Look at me, Rainbow."

She blinked at him as a shiver ran down her body.

"Do you want Daddy to make you feel good, Little girl?"

She nodded, pursing her lips.

"I need words, baby."

She swallowed. "Please, Daddy. Please touch me."

He leaned closer until his lips touched hers, taking her mouth in a sweet, soft, slow, gentle kiss. Seconds later, his fingers found her folds and he stroked through her wetness, making her moan into his mouth.

She arched her chest toward him, her nipples sharp points that brushed against his chest through the T-shirt. Her fingers dug into his shoulders deeper, as if she needed to hold on. It seemed like she might spin out of control.

She'd never been this aroused with any other man before.

When he found her clit and circled it, she moaned against his lips.

He eased his face back slightly. "I love that sound, Little girl. Do it again." He finished that sentence while easing a finger into her channel.

Her eyes rolled back. "Daddy..."

"Even better," he murmured. "You're so wet. Are you always this responsive?"

She shook her head. "No. It's you."

"I like that." His voice was soft, more of a murmur. "Can you come on Daddy's fingers or do you need more stimulation than that?"

She gripped his hip with her knee as he added a finger and rubbed her clit with his thumb. There was no way she could respond. Her brain wasn't sending messages to her mouth.

He chuckled and thrust again, tapping her clit several times. "Come for your Daddy, Little girl. I want to watch you."

She moaned as the tight ball of need in her belly exploded, her orgasm shaking her body, the pulses gripping his fingers.

He thrust faster at first and then slowed as she floated back into herself and blinked at him. A flush covered her cheeks, heating them once again.

"That was so beautiful, Rainbow." He kissed her cheek and then nibbled a path to her ear.

She released his shoulder to run her hand down his biceps, intent on wrapping her palm around his erection, but he removed his hand from her pussy and caught her hand in his. Her wetness coated his fingers, and he brought their combined hands to his mouth to lick his fingers and hers together.

49

She shuddered. The moment was so intimate and intense. "Daddy, can I touch you now?"

"Nope. Not this morning."

"Why not?"

"Because I want you to spend some time learning what it means to be my Little girl first. I want you to feel as certain you're mine as I do. I want you to come to me and know without a doubt that I'm your forever Daddy."

She nodded, shocked by his chivalry. He was serious, and it meant the world to her. No one had ever looked at her the way he was looking at her now. No one had ever been so gentle and loving and nurturing. And certainly no one had ever selflessly given her so much pleasure without wanting something in return.

He lowered her leg from around his hips and kissed her once again. "I bet you're hungry. How about if Daddy makes you breakfast?"

She grinned. "You're going to cook for me?"

He frowned. "Of course I am, Little girl. Often. Especially if you're going to work long hours at your shop. Based on what I've seen so far, you probably lose track of time and don't eat proper meals."

She sighed. "Yeah. That happens. Sometimes I grab a protein shake for lunch."

"Well, I'm going to make you scrambled eggs and bacon. Do you want cheese on them?"

Her eyes went wide. "Yes, please."

"And later this morning, I'll make you a smoothie in the blender for a snack. How does that sound?"

She giggled. "Delicious."

"What time do you have to be at your shop to interview the potential new employees?"

"Not until three."

"So you can spend the day with me until then?"

She nodded.

"Excellent." He patted her bottom. "Go use the bathroom and brush your teeth while I start breakfast."

"I don't have anything to wear, Daddy."

"You don't need anything. I like seeing you in my T-shirt." He wiggled his brows.

"Okay, Daddy." She watched as he released her and rolled off his side of the huge bed. She got a good look at his thick length because he did nothing to hide it, and then she held her breath as she was graced with his fantastic ass as he turned to walk into the bathroom.

Again, how did she get so lucky?

She pinched her arm to make sure she wasn't dreaming. "Ouch," she murmured before sliding off her side of the bed.

Chapter Six

Garrett couldn't stop smiling as he whipped the eggs while the bacon sizzled in the pan. He'd never been more sure of anything in his life. The sweet Little girl singing softly to herself—probably without realizing it—as she entered the kitchen was his.

He glanced at her as she came to him. She'd combed her hair and put it in a high ponytail. He liked it better in two pigtails like she'd worn it at Blaze, but he wouldn't say anything this morning. He didn't want to throw too many things at her at once and risk chasing her away.

After pouring the eggs into a pan, he turned around and lifted her off her feet to set her on one of the stools at the island.

She squealed, her voice making his already stiff cock harder. The dimples on her cheeks were adorable, too. "Daddy, I could have climbed up myself," she admonished as she lifted first one butt cheek then the other to tug his shirt under her bottom.

"I know you could have, but I like doing things for you."

She set one elbow on the island and leaned her chin on her palm. "I like when you do things for me, too." She grinned.

"Orange juice?" he asked.

"Yes, Sir."

He poured her a cup and popped a sippy lid on it before setting it in front of her.

"Why do you have so much stuff for a Little girl, Daddy? Did you have another Little girl living here?"

"Nope. You're the first. But I knew I wanted a special Little girl, so I've been preparing for one for a long time."

"And you think I could be her?" Her eyes were wide and hopeful. Thank God.

"I *know* you're her." He bopped her nose with his finger and turned to stir the eggs and flip the bacon. "Sometimes a Daddy just knows."

"When did you know?"

"When I first walked into your shop and found you singing about frosting, powdered sugar and flour all over your cute body." He turned his head toward her and winked. "You stole my heart that very moment."

Her cheeks flushed adorably. "I was a mess."

"You were a cute mess." He dished up two plates of food and set one in front of her.

"I haven't eaten breakfast in forever. I never have time. I'm always running late."

"Little girl, everyone needs a good breakfast to start the day. Seems like you keep a pretty crazy schedule staying up late and struggling to get out of bed in the morning." He lifted a brow in question as he took a seat next to her, his own plate piled higher with food.

She finished chewing her bite, swallowed, and shrugged. "I used to keep more regular hours when I was living with my grandmother, but since then, I've gotten lazy."

"Sounds like you need a Daddy to help you get on a healthier schedule."

She scrunched up her nose. "That's no fun."

He chuckled. "I bet if you went to bed at a decent hour, you could get up earlier and get your work done during the day so you could sleep at night."

She pushed out her bottom lip in an adorable pout that he was realizing could easily cause her to get wrapped around his finger if he wasn't careful.

He leaned in and took her chin. "If you agree to be my Little girl, I'll have strict rules about bedtimes and meals. You can't go to work on an empty stomach and eat cupcakes all day, Ellie."

She sighed.

He pointed at her plate. "Finish eating. Then you can go explore the nursery. How does that sound?"

She sat up straighter, smiling. "I can't wait." She took her next two bites too close together, stuffing the second one in before swallowing the first.

He grabbed her wrist. "Slow down, Little girl. You'll choke. The toys aren't going anywhere."

"Yes, Sir." Her shoulders dropped as she forced herself to eat slower, but it was hard to keep from chuckling as he watched her struggle.

"Finish your juice." He pointed at her cup and smiled for the millionth time as she lifted it with both hands and tipped it back to suck the juice through the special lid. She was precious and every moment he was more certain he couldn't live without her.

"May I be excused, Daddy?" she asked when her plate was empty.

He lifted her to the floor and patted her bottom. "Go explore... But don't run in the house," he added when she took off at warp speed.

Ten minutes later, he had the kitchen all cleaned up and went in search of her, already missing having her in his sight. He'd be content just watching her play. Even if all he did was sit in the rocking chair in the nursery and keep an eye on her, he would be the happiest man alive.

When he reached the nursery, he stopped in the doorway, his hands on both sides of the frame. His heart nearly leapt out of his chest. She was on her knees in front of the giant dollhouse, moving the little people around. But what made his heart race was the fact that she was talking. Making the little people speak to each other.

"I told you to use both hands, sweetie. Now you've spilled your milk." She danced the mom figure over to the little boy in the kitchen.

"I'm sorry, mommy."

"Do you need mommy to put a sippy lid on your cup?"

"Yes, please."

Garrett couldn't breathe as he watched Ellie so comfortable and happy in his home, in his nursery. She was wearing nothing more than his T-shirt, and even though he couldn't see her bottom, he knew it was bare under the hem.

As she rocked from knee to knee on the plush carpet, she moved the little people around, switching to the daddy and the little girl. "Do you want to sit on daddy's lap so I can read you a story, honey?"

"Yes, daddy." Ellie made the little girl run over to the daddy and jump onto his lap. It took Ellie a minute to get the dolls situated just right in the rocking chair, but then she handed them a tiny book and said, "Once upon a time..."

Garrett quietly entered the room, not wanting to disturb her but needing to be closer. When he settled in the rocking chair, she glanced at him and grinned. "I love the dollhouse so much, Daddy."

"I'm so glad, Rainbow. Did you want Daddy to read you a book like the daddy in the dollhouse?"

She jumped to her feet. "Really?" Her eyes were wide.

He smiled indulgently. "Of course. Pick one out."

She rushed over to the shelf and scanned the titles, choosing the first book in a series he recognized about the adventures of some baby animals. When she returned to him, he lifted her onto his lap, careful to tuck his shirt under her bottom.

56

"What made you choose this one, Rainbow?" he asked as he kissed her forehead and wrapped his arm around her waist.

She tipped her head back and with every bit of innocence stated, "Because it looks like a long series and I'll have to come over here a lot for you to finish it."

His chest squeezed so tight and he pulled her against him, nearly squishing her. "You may come over here as often as you want, every single day. In fact, whenever you're ready, I'd love for you to stay here permanently."

She leaned back. "That's so fast, Daddy. How do you know that?"

He bopped her nose, loving the way she always squished her face when he did so. "I told you. Daddies just know." He suspected she knew, too. She was just too scared to admit it yet.

He opened the book and started reading, loving the way she snuggled into his chest, drawing her knees up and curling against him. As he read, she even brought her thumb to her mouth and started sucking it. He wasn't sure if she realized it or not, but it was so damn cute.

After a while, her eyes started to droop and he leaned her back to meet her gaze. "You're tired, Little girl. You haven't been getting enough sleep lately. How about if Daddy makes you a smoothie and you go down for a nap?"

She tried to perk up. "I don't nap, Daddy. I have too much to do."

"Well, today you don't have to be at the shop until three. Today you can nap." He used a stern voice as he rose and set her on her feet. "Wait right here. I'll go get you a smoothie."

He had already gathered the ingredients after cleaning up from breakfast, so it took just a few minutes to run the blender and pour the healthy mixture into a sippy cup.

When he rounded the doorway this time, he found her standing with her back to him, staring at the adult-sized changing table. She twisted to face him as he entered.

He waited for her to ask questions, but she apparently chose not to. Instead, she climbed back on to his lap and let him hold the sippy cup to her lips. Her eyes were wide as she started drinking. "Mmm," was the only sound she made, clearly enjoying the drink.

"That was so good," she told him when it was gone. "I think I love having you as a Daddy."

"I'm so glad. Are you ready for a nap, Rainbow?"

She hesitated and then licked her lips. "Do you want me to wear a diaper, Daddy?"

He snuggled her closer and rocked. "I would like that, Little girl. I'd like it if you let Daddy take care of you in every way."

"All the time?" Her eyes were wide again.

"No. Not all the time. Obviously, you must go to work and be in your adult space most of the day. But what if you tried being my Little girl when we're in the house?"

She bit into her lower lip as she contemplated. "I've been your Little girl since we got here last night."

"Yep. But there are a few things I haven't introduced you to yet."

"Like diapers..." She squirmed.

"Yes. Like diapers. Remember how I told you I didn't want you to climb out of your crib? That Daddy wants to put the side up from now on while you sleep?"

"Yes," she whispered.

"Well, I'd like you to wear a diaper when you're in your crib. Would you try that for me?"

"Do you want me to use it, Daddy?" She was trembling.

"Of course. That way when you wake up and need to potty you can just go before Daddy even comes in to get you."

She chewed her lip again, deep in thought. "I'll try wearing it, but I don't know if I want to use it."

"Fair enough. Let's start there. I bet once I get your cute bottom covered, you'll realize how nice it is to let someone else take care of you in that way."

"Maybe..."

He stood, holding her in his arms and walking to the changing table. It was hard to contain how elated he was. He had expected this hurdle to be steeper than it was proving. She'd only been in his home one night and she was at least agreeing to try being younger already for naptime. He would call that a win.

He settled her gently on the changing table and reached across to grab the nylon strap, stretching it across her tummy.

She giggled. "I don't think I'll fall off, Daddy."

"Nope. Not now." He bopped her nose, making her giggle before he stepped to the end of the table and grabbed a diaper. Pushing her T-shirt up, he exposed her fully to his view for the first time.

Her breath hitched as he eased her legs apart. "Spread your knees wide for Daddy."

She whimpered as she did what he asked.

He was pleased to see her pussy was very wet. He lifted her bottom and spread the diaper under her before grabbing a tube of diaper cream.

She made a sweet little mewling sound as he rubbed the ointment between her folds, careful to cover all her soft skin. "There. That will protect my Little girl's bottom." He gave the curls above her mound a playful tug. "Daddy will want to shave this off soon, Rainbow. Diapered girls need to have smooth, naked pussies."

The blush that spread across her cheeks made his heart rate pick up again. "I've never shaved down there before, Daddy. Won't it feel strange?"

"Only for a few days. Then you'll love it. Having a bare pussy will help you get into your Little space, especially when you're diapered."

She didn't answer, but she didn't argue with him either.

As soon as he had her diaper secured around her waist, he unfastened the strap and lifted her into his arms. Cradling her against him, he headed for the crib. "Time for a nap, Rainbow."

He eased her onto her back, pulled the covers over her, and turned toward the shelves. "How about if you pick a friend to sleep with you?"

She twisted her head to the side as he pointed at the row of stuffies on the shelf. "Ummm. The unicorn. It looks like the one you colored for me at Blaze." She kicked her legs adorably under the covers as he brought it to her, and she squeezed the life out of him as soon as he settled the unicorn in her arms.

"What should we name him?" Garrett asked.

"Sprinkles!"

He smiled. "I love that." He leaned over to kiss her forehead. "Sleep tight, Rainbow." He lifted the side of her crib. "And remember, Little girls don't climb out of their cribs. It's not safe. If you need Daddy because you have a tummy ache or you're hurting in some other way, call out. If you need to potty, that's what your diaper is for."

"Yes, Daddy."

He patted her tummy and left the room, but he felt like he left a piece of himself in that nursery with her. She had stolen his heart and it would remain in her possession when he wasn't in the room.

Chapter Seven

Ellie was confused for a moment when she woke up, but she quickly remembered where she was as she glanced around, finding herself in Garrett's nursery for the second time today.

She hugged Sprinkles to her chest and sighed. She couldn't remember when she'd ever been this content. She'd had dreams of one day meeting a Daddy and having the perfect life with him, but she hadn't expected it to actually happen to her.

It was so fast though. Was it real? Could she trust what she was feeling?

She started to sit up and remembered she was wearing a diaper. The thick bulk of it was keeping her legs awkwardly parted.

On top of that, she really needed to pee. She relaxed back onto the mattress and rubbed her cheek with the unicorn's colorful horn, thinking about her options.

She knew Daddy really wanted her to use the diaper. She also knew he wouldn't pressure her if she wasn't ready. Right? She could either ask him to take it off and let her go to the bathroom, or she could pee herself in the crib and endure the embarrassment of being changed.

She imagined his face and how pleased he would be if she

wet her diaper without being prodded. Was it that big of a deal? He didn't seem to think so. He'd made it clear that as her Daddy, he really preferred that she wet herself. He wanted to take care of her in every way, including that rather personal manner.

She gritted her teeth as the need to pee grew stronger and finally made the decision to just do it. Try it out. If she didn't like it, she didn't have to do it again.

It took a minute to convince her bladder to let go while lying in bed, but finally she succeeded, discovering that it was actually kind of liberating in a way. There was no pressure to leap out of bed and run to the bathroom. It was just a wet diaper. He would whisk it off, dispose of it, and it would be over.

It was not, however, comfortable as soon as she filled it, and she winced at the wet feeling as she squirmed. "Daddy?" she called out in a soft voice.

She was kind of surprised when he immediately showed up. Her voice hadn't been that loud. "Hey there, Little girl." He was grinning wide as he lowered the side of the crib and set his hand on her tummy, rubbing her gently. "Did you have a nice nap, baby?"

"Yes, Sir. How did you hear me?"

He pointed at a small white box clipped to the side of the crib. "Baby monitor. I had the other part next to me in the living room."

"Oh."

He pulled the covers back and slid his hand down to pat the front of her diaper. His smile broadened as she'd expected. "I'm so proud of you, Rainbow."

"Thank you, Daddy."

He scooped her up in his arms and carried her to the changing table. After securing her once again, he quickly removed the diaper and wiped her clean with no fuss. "You still have an hour or so before we need to go to your apartment and get you some new clothes to wear to your shop. Do you want to wear a fresh diaper until then?"

She thought about his suggestion. "Do you want me to, Daddy?" She decided she didn't mind and she really liked to please him.

"I would love nothing more than for you to spend as much time diapered in my home as you're comfortable with. It tells me you trust me to take care of you. But I know it's a huge step and I won't push you if you're not ready."

She chewed on her lip as she thought about his request. "I think I could try it this time, Daddy." It was only an hour. She wouldn't need to use it in that time. But she could see how it felt. It wouldn't be the same as when she was lying in the crib. It would feel strange and awkward between her legs.

"Good girl. If you don't like it, you tell Daddy, okay?"

She nodded.

As he slid a clean diaper under her, she watched him closely. Everything he did was so intimate. So caring. She felt cherished in a way she'd never imagined. Her belly did flip flops as he spread more diaper cream on her folds and secured her at the waist.

If that was how it was going to feel to be treasured like she was a precious jewel, she might get used to being Daddy's Little girl after all. Ellie lifted her arms, silently asking him to pick her up. To her delight, her Daddy scooped her from the tall changing table and held her close to his chest. As if he didn't want to be separated from her, Garrett strolled back and forth across the floor.

"How do you feel, Rainbow?" he asked softly as he walked.

"I feel really good." Ellie hesitated before adding, "I like being here with you."

His hand fondly patted her diapered bottom. "I like having you here, too. Are you awake enough to work on the rules we need to guide us?"

PEPPER NORTH & PAIGE MICHAELS

"Rules? Like what I'll get spanked for?" she asked, leaning slightly away to study his face.

"There are other consequences you might earn other than spankings."

"Like what?" she asked, fascinated by the thought of her stern Daddy's plans.

"Standing in the corner, losing playtime, writing sentences. Your misbehavior will tell me what you need to make better choices. These rules will include what you need to feel safe here," he added.

"Daddies have rules?"

"Good Daddies always have rules. Let's go work at the counter. I have some paper set up there."

"Okay," she agreed, eager to see what he had in mind.

"Oh!" Ellie gasped as her Daddy slid her down the length of his body until her feet touched the soft carpet. There was no doubt that taking care of her so intimately had turned Garrett on. The proof of his attraction tented his pants. Ellie tried not to stare but she knew what the fabric covered.

"Eyes on mine, Little girl," Garrett ordered in a husky voice.

Ellie jerked her head back to meet his gaze as her face heated with embarrassment. "Sorry," she whispered.

"Never be sorry that we're attracted to each other. I'm not."

Garrett took her hand and led her to the kitchen. He walked slowly as Ellie waddled uncertainly due to the thick padding between her thighs. She looked up at him repeatedly to make sure he wasn't laughing at her. Each time, he squeezed her hand in encouragement.

When they reached the kitchen, he helped boost her up on to the stool before sitting next to her. Ellie squirmed a bit on the padding. It wasn't uncomfortable—maybe her spanked bottom didn't ache as bad when she sat on her diaper?

"Here are the things I'm going to require you do." Garrett put a piece of paper in front of her. He paused as she read.

. . .

Daddy's Rules for Ellie

1. Always tell Daddy the truth.
2. Eat and drink healthy things every day.
3. Go to bed at _____ and wake up at _____.
4. Spend time with Daddy every day.
5. Practice safety at work and home.

"There aren't any times here?" she pointed out.

"What time do you need to be at Little Cakes to be ready to open?" Garrett probed.

"I'll need to be there super early—especially in the beginning until I have a routine. Maybe four am?"

"That is early. I didn't fill in times because we need to work backward from the time you need to wake up to make sure you sleep eight hours each night. It takes fifteen minutes to get to the store from here. How long does it take from your apartment?"

"Five."

"How long do you need to get ready?"

"Five minutes to get dressed and wash my face."

"And eat."

"That takes too long. I'll eat midmorning after the rush dies out."

"No. You'll eat in the morning to give you energy for the day."

Ellie stared at him. There was no wiggle room at all in his words. "I don't like to eat in the morning." She recalled he had warned her this morning he would expect her to eat breakfast.

"Then you'll have a smoothie with some fruit and yogurt."

"That doesn't sound too bad," she relented. "I don't like melons."

"A smoothie without melons, check. You can drink that on your way if you or I make it the night before. So, you'll need to wake up at three-forty at home or three-thirty here." Garrett filled in the earlier time on the rule sheet.

"To get eight hours of sleep, you'll need to be tucked in bed by seven-thirty," he pointed out and completed the sheet.

"I can't go to bed at that time. It won't even be dark!" she pointed out indignantly.

"I'll buy some blackout curtains for the nursery," he answered.

"No one goes to bed at seven-thirty!" she insisted.

"A Little girl who wakes up at three in the morning does."

"What happens if I don't?"

"I'll spank your bottom and put you in bed," Garrett warned with a steely look.

Ellie watched him fill in the early bedtime. *I'll never be able to do that.* She knew herself too well. "I don't really need eight hours of sleep. I'm good on five."

"That's not going to happen as long as I'm in your life, Little girl."

Staring at him, Ellie shrugged. "You can lock me in the crib, but you can't make me go to sleep."

"Challenge accepted, Rainbow."

Chapter Eight

Unlocking the front door, Ellie let herself into Little Cakes. After a stop at her apartment to jump into fresh clothes, Garrett dropped her off half an hour before her first interview. She looked around at the café-style chairs and tables scattered strategically around the dining room. It looked inviting in the charming space.

"People are going to love it here!" she announced aloud.

"They really are!" a familiar voice responded from behind her.

Whirling, Ellie relaxed to see Riley in the doorway. "Hi! You're early. Come on in."

Ellie waved the dark-haired woman with the pale-blue eyes inside and asked her to sit at the nearest table. "I'll be right back." She ducked through the swinging door and grabbed a plate of assorted cupcakes and two small bottles of milk.

Tucking her clipboard of official questions the internet told her she should ask under her arm, Ellie balanced the treats as she returned to Riley. "I thought you should sample a cupcake to make sure you can endorse them."

"They're beautiful. I'd love to try one," Riley said eagerly. Carefully, she plucked a red velvet cupcake from the platter.

After peeling back the paper, Riley took a big bite, smearing the cream cheese frosting on her upper lip and even on her nose.

"Mmm!" she hummed, casually wiping the frosting from her face.

"Good, huh? That's one of my favorites, too." Ellie laughed at herself. "I'm not making anything I don't like."

"If everything is as good as this is, you're going to make a million dollars!" Riley complimented.

Ellie watched her look at the top of the cupcake. Riley rotated it slowly as she stared at the beautiful frosting on top. "Tell me what you're thinking?"

"I chose this one because my grandma adored red velvet cake. She'd had one for her wedding because grandpa canceled the plain white cake her parents had ordered to save money and changed it to this yummy concoction. There's a picture in her wedding album of them cutting the cake. The excitement on her face is priceless."

"That's a sweet story," Ellie mused.

"She always said she noticed what looked like a sprinkling of red velvet crumbs in a lovely pattern on the top of the cake. But she figured the baker had added those as a free gift for her wedding day. Grandma always told me to find a man who notices the small things that make me happy."

Ellie smiled.

Riley paused to study the plain, cream-colored frosting on top. "You could add some sprinkles of red velvet crumbs on the cupcake to clue in people who don't know what it is. Maybe on one half?" she suggested.

Leaning forward to look at the icing pattern she'd decided on for those cupcakes, Ellie suggested, "Or maybe a swirl?"

"Can you do that? That would be unique."

"If you come work for me, I'll teach you how to do that!" Ellie returned the grin on Riley's face.

"I brought the application from the website," Riley said, pulling the folded sheets from her purse.

"I already know you have the skills to talk to customers politely and work a register and a credit card machine," Ellie said with a smile as she accepted the wrinkled sheets. "You're already working. Do you need another job?"

"Yes. I'm saving up for something important."

"Riley, are you going to quit when you have enough money?" Ellie forced herself to ask. She wanted to have some people she could rely on, especially in the beginning.

"I like working. If I meet that goal, I'll set another. I promise you, Ellie, I won't leave you in a lurch."

"Then unless you're a serial killer or allergic to sprinkles, you've got a job."

"Thanks, Ellie! I promise I'll work hard."

Ellie picked up her bottle of milk and toasted Riley before taking a drink.

Trying not to make snap judgements, Ellie considered all the applicants with an open mind. She carefully selected two other women to work part time with Riley. With two people to work the front and Ellie baking in the back and helping out during rushes, she thought they could handle just about anything.

Her advertised time for interviews was almost over. The platter of cupcakes had dwindled as each candidate had eagerly enjoyed one. Ellie wrinkled her nose at the thought of the lady who stated she didn't eat sugar and actually called it evil. When Ellie had suggested that her body would absorb demonic sugar as it landed on her skin in the sweet shop, the woman had quickly decided to withdraw her application.

"Why did she even come?" Ellie wondered out loud.

A deep rumble of laughter made her look up. A familiar huge figure stood inside the doorway. Ellie realized her question could have a variety of interpretations. Quickly, she covered her embarrassment with chatter.

"Hi, Bear. Want a cupcake?"

"Yes. I'd love one. Maybe after you interview me?" he suggested.

"You're here for an interview?" Ellie asked in confusion. The large man served as one of the dungeon masters for Blaze. She'd never wondered what his real job was. Bear hadn't been around for long. He fit so well into the club vibe that it just felt like he'd been there forever.

"Yes." Bear settled into one of the chairs Garrett had constructed. Suddenly, Ellie was glad her Daddy had put them together. He was a big man. Those screws needed to be secure.

"Here's my application," Bear broke the silence to hand her the crisp sheets of paper.

Ellie glanced over the application and her eyes stuck on one word, baker. "You want to make cupcakes with me?" she asked in disbelief.

"I do. I just left the military. I began as a culinary specialist and worked my way up into catering for special events. My specialty was in pastries and desserts."

"You're kidding? With your experience, you could open your own shop," Ellie pointed out, flabbergasted.

"I don't want to hassle with all the business stuff. I just want to come in and make pretty cupcakes."

Looking at the extremely muscular man, Ellie swallowed hard and tried to sound very in charge. "It's my kitchen. I'm the boss. Everything goes the way I want it to go."

"Definitely. At Little Cakes, you are the decision maker. I'll reserve the right to make suggestions," Bear answered without a trace of annoyance or disagreement.

"I can live with that. Pick a cupcake and tell me what improvements you'd make." Ellie offered him the plate that now held just a few delights. To her surprise, she watched him select the plainest one—simple yellow cake with chocolate icing.

Bear stripped off the icing and took a big bite. "Mmm!" he

74

hummed as he chewed the first bite. Swallowing, he looked over the small cake before meeting her gaze.

"This is a damn fine product. You used butter, extra eggs, and milk. People will go wild over these. There's only one thing you might try to see if it gives it one hint of a boost. Ever added a quick brush of simple syrup to the top before frosting?"

"Just to add moisture?" she asked, leaning in.

"A bit. People like a little bling with their cupcakes. I'm pretty good with chocolate. We could make a small rectangle from chocolate and use gold leaf to add the words *Little Cakes*," he suggested.

"And, stick that in the frosting at the top? We'd need really good dark chocolate," she stressed, turning over a spare job application to make notes. "What tools do you need to work with the chocolate base?"

"You'll have to hire me first," he said with a big grin that transformed his face from stern and unyielding to devastatingly handsome.

"Wow! I wasn't expecting that!" Ellie sat back against her chair in astonishment at the change in his appearance.

"What?"

"You just went from serious bouncer man to gorgeous muffin man in less than a second," Ellie blurted.

"Muffin man... Only a Little..." Bear shook his head as he continued to smile. "So, when do I start?"

"Let's go make a batch of cupcakes. See how we work together. We'll try out your suggestion minus the chocolate bling." Ellie stood and motioned for Bear to come with her. To her astonishment, the large man walked over to lock the outer door.

"Do all Daddies have a lock fetish?" she asked.

"It's part of Daddy school. Lesson one—make sure Littles are safe," Bear answered with a wink.

"Are you going to be a grumpy bear at Blaze still or will I see the teddy bear there now that I've seen the relaxed side of you?"

she asked, leading the way into the back. Ellie threw him a clean apron from the stack by the racks. As he unfolded it, she zinged a hair net his way like a rubber band. To her delight, Bear snatched it out of the air like a pro baseball player.

She giggled as she gathered ingredients and showed him where she'd organized everything. Soon, Ellie watched Bear sift the dry ingredients together with an approving smile. He did know the tricks to produce a delicate, tender cupcake.

As they waited for the first batch to bake, Ellie pulled out a cooled batch of chocolate cupcakes from the walk-in. "I've got these. I wanted to experiment a bit with how to jazz them up. I thought maybe a mint zing like those layered chocolates?"

"A bunch of people do chocolate mint flavors. Anything with a coffee embellishment is a big hit now. What would you think about an expresso flavor?" he suggested.

"I like the idea. What do you think? Put expresso powder in the frosting?"

"That could be amazing. I'd test two versions to see what's most popular. Filled and non-filled. I don't know how coffee flavored your customers would like it. You could fill with the same frosting or maybe a more subtle flavor inside like a cookies and cream version? Maybe decorate with chocolate covered expresso beans."

"Let's try a couple of versions and see what we think? Anything coffee will pull in the teens and twenty somethings." Ellie clapped her hands in enthusiasm.

She hadn't had someone to bounce ideas off in the kitchen since her grandmother had passed away. Ellie wasn't sad. She was totally jazzed. Her grandmother was watching from heaven with the biggest smile. Who knows—maybe she was the one who sent Bear?

Two hours later, Ellie set half a cupcake down with a sigh. "Those are incredible. I don't think I've ever tasted a flavor like that. What are we going to call it?"

"Mochalicious? Cookies and Cafe? No, that's not right. We'll have to come up with a better name," Bear suggested.

He looked over the display of rejected, half-eaten cupcakes. "I'm going to have to run for miles to burn off all these calories."

"I'll add a new pair of sneakers to your salary," Ellie suggested with a grin.

"I've got the job?"

"I'd tackle you if you tried to get out of here now. I enjoyed baking with you. Thanks for joining my team, Bear."

"My pleasure, Little girl. You're going to keep me on my toes. I'm looking forward to it. When do I start?"

"The grand opening is in four days. The front shop staff starts training tomorrow. Would you begin the day after that? That will give me a full day to work with them and then we can start baking. It would help if this week you came in Tuesday and Wednesday before the grand opening on Thursday."

"How many days do you want me to work? I'm at Blaze on Wednesday, Friday, and Saturday evenings. I'm assuming you'll start baking early in the morning. If you need me the mornings that follow, I can come here when the club closes and get the first batches in the oven."

"I'm afraid I don't know how much help I'll need or which days. Could we start with three days a week? I think I'll need to increase the days you're here as I build up the clientele," Ellie suggested, holding her breath. Now that she'd seen him in action, Ellie knew Bear could get a job anywhere. He was that good. To her relief, Bear nodded.

"I'll have to get another job in a few weeks if you don't need me full time," he warned. "That will make my schedule less flexible, but I'll give you priority on which days you need me to work."

"Deal!" Ellie announced, extending her hand to shake on the agreement.

Chapter Nine

After parking his SUV, Garrett walked up to the front door of Little Cakes. He could see the lights on in the kitchen through the swinging door. The dining room was completely black. Reaching a hand out to try the handle, Garrett breathed out a sigh of relief when the door rattled. Ellie had listened and locked the door.

He pulled his phone from his pocket and called her. Faintly, Garrett heard music playing from inside. Pressing his ear to the glass door, he heard a familiar tune by a country singer questioning someone's choice of a Daddy. Garrett felt his lips part in a wide grin. His Little had customized his ring tone.

Shaking his head, Garrett knocked loudly on the glass. His Rainbow had locked the door but left her phone abandoned at one of the tables out front. He paused and knocked again. The swinging door moved slightly as someone from the kitchen peeked out. In a burst of energy, Ellie ran to unlock the door.

"Hi!" she chirped after she opened the door. Starting forward, she suddenly halted uncertainly.

"I've been away from you for hours. Could a needy Daddy get a hug?" Garrett prompted.

"Yes!" Ellie launched herself into his arms, hugging him tightly.

"I missed you, Little girl," Garrett whispered before kissing her deeply. Sweet flavors of chocolate, buttercream, and vanilla tantalized him. He loved Ellie's own delicious flavor even more than the ingredients she had sampled. Remembering the wide expanse of windows behind him, Garrett reined in his greeting.

Ellie blinked a few times when he lifted his mouth from hers. Garrett loved that she needed a few seconds to recover. When she licked her lips, Garrett couldn't resist kissing her again. This time when he pulled himself away, he asked, "Did you miss me, Rainbow?"

"So much!"

"Tell me how your interviews went."

"For the counter, I hired Riley—you know her from Blaze. Tori and Sue are my other hires. Tori is quiet but I can already tell she'll be reliable and helpful. My last pick was Sue. She's in her thirties and is a super cheerful. Lark promised to come help in the beginning when we're overrun by cupcake starving hordes of people."

"Lark Adams?" Garrett asked, remembering the name from the contract Ellie had signed. *There can't be that many women named Lark.*

"Yes. She's my best friend in the world. She helped me find this place. Lark is the best realtor."

"She is a good friend to come help out," he agreed with a smile.

"Guess who came to interview for the baker's job?" Ellie asked, bouncing on her toes in excitement.

"Your second-best friend?" Garrett teased.

"No! Bear from Blaze!"

"Bear is a baker?" Garrett questioned.

"He is and he has good ideas. We're trying to think of a name for a cream-filled chocolate cupcake we created with an expresso flavor." Ellie looked at him expectantly.

"Not my specialty, Little girl, but I'll try to come up with something," he promised. "Right now, I want to take you home. Are you at a good place to stop for the evening?"

"I just need to turn off the dishwasher and wipe down the counters."

Garrett's phone rang and he checked the screen to see if he needed to answer. "Go. Take your time. I need to take this call."

"This is Garrett Erickson," he identified himself for the answering service he used for his commercial properties business. As the efficient woman relayed the message, Garrett watched his Little skip happily into the kitchen to close it down for the night. When she disappeared from his view, Garrett forced himself to concentrate.

By the time, he'd finished, Ellie swept through the swinging door with her keys. "I'm ready!"

"Grab your phone," he directed, pointing at the table.

"Oh! I wondered where that was. Look! You called me," Ellie exclaimed, turning the screen toward him.

"I hope I'm the only one who warranted that song choice," Garrett admonished as he ushered her to the door. To his delight, he watched her cheeks become rosy.

"Um, just you... It seemed appropriate."

"I'm glad you know I'm your Daddy. We have just enough time to have dinner, a warm bath, and maybe story time before bedtime."

"I'll start going to bed early when I open the shop," Ellie decided.

"No way. Little girls need a regular routine." Garrett helped Ellie into his SUV.

"I don't have to always do what you say," she answered stubbornly.

"Of course not. You are welcome to choose to experience a consequence." Garrett closed the door with a soft click and walked around the hood of the SUV. He slid into the driver's seat and started the engine before looking over at Ellie.

"No, thank you," she said politely as she scratched at a splotch of dried batter that clung to her leggings.

"Smart choice," Garrett commented, covering her busy fingers with his free hand. He squeezed her hand when she turned to press her palm to his.

"I'm headed to your apartment. I'd like you to pack a bag of necessities to stay with me tonight. Are you ready to stay with Daddy?"

Without hesitating even a second, Ellie nodded, looking down at their intertwined hands.

"Use your words, Rainbow."

"Yes, Daddy. I want to stay with you." Ellie peeked up at him.

He knew his Little girl needed reassurance. "That makes my heart happy. I want you with me."

The corners of her lips tilted upward in an instantly addictive smile. He wanted to see her this happy every day. Making a vow to keep his Little girl grinning, Garrett navigated the short distance to Ellie's apartment.

Just as she had that morning, Ellie suggested, "I'll just run up by myself and grab what I need. My place is a mess."

Garrett debated forcing the issue to accompany her. He didn't believe that a simple mess of clothes on the floor or dirty dishes in the sink were the true reason she preferred him to wait in the SUV. "You're not hiding another man up there, are you?"

"No, Daddy," Ellie denied with wide eyes as she vigorously shook her head.

"What is it you don't want me to see?" Garrett asked.

After several long seconds, she caved. "You can come up with me."

Garrett switched off the SUV. "Let me open your door, Rainbow." He watched her as he circled the hood. Ellie looked like she was giving herself a pep talk. *What am I going to find in her apartment?*

After opening her door, Garrett helped her out and held on

to her hand. They walked together to the entrance. He was pleased to see she had to let herself into the apartment complex with her key. Only residents could access the brightly lit corridors. Garrett followed her up two flights of stairs.

Ellie paused in front of a closed door. She turned back to look at Garrett. He brushed the hair from her face and cupped her jaw with his immense hand.

"I promise you that whatever you're concerned about will be okay."

"Anything?" she questioned.

"Anything."

Ellie turned the doorknob and pushed open the door. Garrett stepped in and looked around. Everything was perfectly tidy. The only thing that caught his eyes was the appalling wallpaper. It didn't seem to have a repeatable pattern but was completely random. Curious, he stepped toward the closest wall and stopped as Ellie darted forward to stand in front of him.

"I had permission to decorate."

Garrett looked over her head and everything clicked into place. Stickers! She had plastered the walls of the main living space with multicolored bedazzlements celebrating everything from cartoons to brand names. Only small portions of the plastered surface peeked through. It must have taken her hours to arrange all of these.

Enchanted, he felt his lips curve into a grin. "Looks like I need to create a space for you to make your own in the nursery. That is if you have any more?"

"Oh, I have more. I like stickers."

"I can see that. Is this what you didn't want me to see?" he asked, trying to sober his expression so she wouldn't think he was laughing at her. Garrett definitely wasn't! He found Ellie completely adorable.

"Yes?" she hesitantly answered. "You mean it's okay if I put some on the walls at your house?"

"If this makes you happy, Little girl, I'll come up with something that will allow you to be creative and quiet the old man inside me who might protest."

"There's not an old man inside you, is there? I haven't seen him." Ellie's mouth rounded in a silent O. He could tell she was remembering her spanking when she snuck one hand around her side to rub on her bottom.

"That's not the old man, Rainbow. That's the Daddy."

When she nodded with a serious expression, Garrett encouraged. "Go pack clothes for several days."

"Can I bring my stuffie?" she whispered as her face blossomed with an embarrassed pink tinge.

"Of course. That's perfect. I can't wait to meet him or her," Garrett assured his Little girl.

"His name is Cuddles. He's a puppy," Ellie provided over her shoulder as she walked quickly into the bedroom.

Garrett settled on the couch to wait patiently. Without a speck of hesitation, he eavesdropped as Ellie shared the news with Cuddles that they were going on a great adventure. His lips curved into a wide smile as she told him about Sprinkles who was super sweet.

Take things slowly, he tried to counsel himself and knew he wasn't going to take his own advice. He was already too far gone.

"Let's go to the nursery," Garrett suggested as he led Ellie down the hallway. He set her small rolling suitcase by the closet before picking her up in his arms for a squeeze and a quick kiss. He knew routines were important for Little girls. He'd help Ellie adjust into Littlespace each evening with a change in clothing.

Before she could protest, he laid her on the changing table and whisked off her flour-dusted sneakers. Garrett hooked his fingers into the waistband of her pants and began to tug Ellie's panties and leggings down.

"Daddy?" she asked, wrapping her fingers around his hands to hold them in place.

"When you're at home, I need to take care of my Little girl. You've been big all day. I think it's time to be Little now."

Garrett watched her process his words. Slowly her hands relaxed around his and she lifted her arms to cover her face. "That's right, Rainbow. Keep that light out of your eyes," he suggested, giving her an alternative to hiding.

"It's bright!" she whispered as he tugged the clothing over her feet and dropped everything on the floor.

Making a mental note to get a hamper for the nursery, Garrett wrapped his fingers around her ankles and lifted her hips up to slide a thick diaper underneath Ellie's bottom. Settling her softly down onto the padding, he spread her legs and grabbed a heated wipe. Garrett brushed the soft material across her pink folds, allowing his fingers to caress her intimately. Her body responded immediately to his touch as slick juices gathered. When her pelvis rose repeatedly to press against his caresses, Garrett pulled the front of the diaper into place and secured it snuggly around her.

"Daddy!" she protested, looking at him in disbelief.

"Playtime later. It's time for dinner now." Garrett lifted her from the table to stand next to him.

"Let's get this dirty shirt off. Arms up," he instructed. As she tried to adjust from the hint of pleasure, Garrett stripped off her T-shirt and bra. Taking her hand, he led her from the nursery.

"I need a shirt, Daddy," Ellie protested, digging in her heels as she covered her plump breasts with her arms.

"It's just Daddy and his Little girl here. Are you cold?"

"No," she admitted.

"Then come sit at the table, Rainbow, while I fix us something to eat. This way you won't get anything dirty as you munch." He tugged on her hand and was delighted as she obediently followed him down the hall.

"I'm hungry. Are you?" Garrett urged as he set her down in her fresh diaper.

"I ate a lot of cupcakes this afternoon with Bear," Ellie confessed.

"Once you get your menu set, you won't have to sample so many. I know it's fun and filling to taste test everything. What was your favorite?" Garrett distracted her as he wrapped his arms around her ribcage to boost her up into the highchair. Quickly, he fastened the tray to secure Ellie in place.

"Chocolate cream-filled," she answered absent-mindedly as she ran her hand over the tray in front of her. "This wasn't here this morning, Daddy."

"My Little girl needed her own special place to sit at the table," he answered as he pulled out eggs, milk, flour, and oil.

Chapter Ten

Ellie giggled. "What are you making, Daddy?"

He glanced at her with a wink. "Breakfast for dinner. Do pancakes sound good?"

She swung her legs out and back a few times. "Yes. I love breakfast for dinner."

"Me too. It's easy and filling, especially on nights when I haven't had a chance to figure out a dinner plan." He poured her a cup of milk and popped a sippy lid on it before handing it to her. "Drink this while I cook."

He tickled her neck before returning to the stove, making her scrunch her head down to her shoulder in a fit of giggles. It felt weird sitting in the kitchen without a shirt on, and she had to grip the sides of the tray to keep from covering her boobs.

Garrett acted like it wasn't the least bit unusual for her to be sitting in his kitchen in an adult-sized high chair wearing nothing but a diaper.

Part of her was still uncertain about this arrangement and the level of submission he expected from her as his Little, but another part of her loved every second of it. The way he pampered and took care of her. The way he glanced at her every few seconds as if to make sure she was still there—safe and content.

She was beyond safe and content. There was very little that could possibly happen to her while she was secured in this seat. She supposed she could choke on the milk if it went down the wrong pipe, but otherwise, it wasn't as though she were small enough to slide down under the tray and fall to the floor.

Her cheeks heated more every time he looked though, his obvious concern and devotion warming her through and through.

When he was finished cooking, he set a plate on her high chair tray. It was bright pink with separate compartments he'd filled with bite-sized pieces of buttered pancakes, syrup, and apple sauce. He also handed her a napkin and an adult-sized chubby toddler fork.

She lifted it, giggling again. "Where do you find so many things for adult Littles, Daddy?"

He grinned as he settled in his seat at the table next to her. "There are online shops for just about anything, Rainbow, and these days even a few brick-and-mortar stores."

She dipped a pancake piece into the syrup and popped it into her mouth. "Delicious," she announced before swallowing.

"Don't talk with your mouth full, Little one."

"Sorry, Daddy," she murmured before taking another bite. She realized she wouldn't ordinarily ever speak with food in her mouth. Not in her adult persona. But something happened when she was with him, especially when they were alone in his home. It was like a switch flipped and she became Little the moment they entered the house. Even the most basic behaviors reverted to those of a younger age.

He gave one of her big toes a tug. "You're absolutely precious, Rainbow."

She sat up straighter at the compliment and finished eating her dinner.

After Daddy loaded the dishwasher, he declared, "Bath time and then story time and bedtime for you."

She glanced at the windows. It was still daylight. It would be strange going to bed this early. She couldn't imagine how she would manage to sleep eight hours like he insisted, but she would try. For him. Without fussing.

Garrett wiped her face and hands before removing the tray and lifting her from the highchair.

She wobbled a bit when he set her on her feet, unaccustomed to the awkward bulk of a diaper between her legs.

"Careful there, Rainbow." He patted her bottom and then took her hand in his to lead her toward the bathroom. After sitting on the toilet seat, he reached between her legs and pressed his hand against her pussy through the diaper.

Her breath hitched and she reached out to grab his knee as she swayed toward him. Even through the thick absorbent material, his touch aroused her.

"Do you need to use your diaper before I remove it, Little one? You're totally dry."

She shook her head. No way was she ready to pee herself standing in front of him. She was far too self-conscious. "No, Sir," she murmured.

He lifted her chin with his free hand and narrowed his gaze at her. "Are you sure? You haven't gone since I picked you up from work."

She nodded. "I'm sure." But all this talk about peeing caused her to feel the increased pressure, and she started shifting her weight back and forth from one leg to the other.

"Ellie..." he warned. "Talk to me. I can see that you need to go."

She swallowed. "Can I just use the potty this time, Daddy? I'm not ready to use a diaper in front of you."

He nodded. "Yes, Little girl. You may. What you may not do is lie to Daddy. Understood? Honesty is the only way for this relationship to work. If I ask you to do something you're not ready for, you need to tell me. We've talked about what I expect from you in the long run. You know Daddy would like to take care of you completely when we're at home. But I also know I'm throwing a lot at you all at once. If you're uncomfortable with anything, you need to say so and I'll adjust." He lifted a brow.

She threw her arms around his neck and kissed his cheek. "Thank you, Daddy. Please could I just have a moment of privacy to use the potty then, Daddy?"

He stood and bent down to kiss her forehead. "You may." Before leaving her, he removed her diaper and rolled it up to put it in the trash, leaving her naked.

"I'll be back in a few minutes to give you a bath." He stroked her cheek and eased from the room, shutting the door with a soft click.

Ellie quickly peed, flushed, and washed her hands. While she went through the motions, she felt lonely and a little uneasy. Maybe it would have been easier to just use the diaper like Daddy preferred. It would please him. She knew that. He'd already made that clear when he'd changed her after her nap.

She glanced at the toilet, knowing she wouldn't be sitting on it very often in the future. If ever.

Daddy knocked on the door softly. "Can I come back in, Rainbow?"

"Yes, Sir."

He was smiling as he returned and didn't say a word about her choice to use the potty. He simply turned on the water in the tub, adjusted the temperature, and put the stopper in the bottom.

As it filled, he lifted her into the tub. "On your bottom, Little one."

She sat, noticing for the first time the new additions to the bathroom. There were bath toys and crayons in the corners of the tub. Her face lit up as she reached for the chubby colored crayons. "What are these for, Daddy?"

"They're for coloring on the walls of the tub." He tapped her nose. "They wash right off." He poured some baby soap onto a washcloth while she twisted toward the tile and drew a smiley face.

Daddy reached around to wash her arms while still letting her color between strokes. "Be sure you use these special crayons on the tile walls and only in the tub, Rainbow."

She glanced at him. "Yes, Sir."

"I know you like to be creative. I'll come up with a place where you can use your stickers and other art supplies in the nursery. Until then, you can color in the tub."

She grinned. "Okay, Daddy." It warmed her heart that he was so thoughtful about her creative side. When she was at work, she could apply her skills to her cupcakes, but at home, she really did like to color and play with stickers.

The fact that she'd started covering her walls had happened by accident. One day, she'd been eating a banana at the kitchen counter. She had peeled off the Chiquita sticker and absentmindedly stuck it to the wall next to her. It made her laugh, so she'd left it there and done it again the next day with an apple. Inspired, she'd started purchasing stickers. Pretty ones. Colorful ones. And the wall of stickers came to life.

It was fun and playful and made her smile every time she came home. If Daddy gave her a place like that in his house, she would be the happiest Little girl in the world.

Ellie wiggled happily as he stroked the soft bath pouf down her back. What a treat to have someone taking care of her. Her breath caught in her throat as the soft material glanced over the sensitive swell of one breast as he washed her side. She hadn't considered how arousing being bathed would be. How intimately would he touch her?

The moment that question formed in Ellie's mind, she knew the answer. This was her Daddy. He would make sure that she was clean everywhere.

"Breathe, Little one," the handsome man reminded her as he washed her throat and across her collarbones.

Looking up to meet his gaze, Ellie followed his instructions and took a deep breath. She froze in place as his hand glided the soapy pouf over her breasts. The air gushed from her lungs as he circled one full mound and brushed over one nipple. It tightened almost painfully in reaction to his touch.

He didn't dally as she would have liked. Ellie squeezed her inner thighs, trying to control the intimate heat gathering between her legs. When Garrett picked up a cup and dipped it into the water to pour it slowly over her skin to rinse off the suds, Ellie tried to conceal her arousal by turning to the tile to color once again.

She'd almost restrained her desire when he set the cup down with a click. He only had her lower half to wash. Her Daddy would know how much she reacted to his touch when he cleaned between her legs!

Ellie jumped when Garrett lifted one foot from the water. She kept her eyes fixed on the colorful wall as she tried to concentrate on something else. His hands swept the soft material over her foot and between her toes.

"Ooh!" Ellie moaned in delight before she could stop herself.

"My Little girl likes to be clean," Garrett celebrated as he washed her calf and moved to her thigh.

Focusing on breathing, Ellie tried to inhale and exhale normally as his touch reached between her legs.

"Wait!" burst from her lips as he shifted to wash her other foot.

His deep chuckle clued her in that she'd said that aloud. "Later, Rainbow. Perhaps you'll have a special bedtime story."

Wondering if he could be suggesting a different activity other than reading, Ellie watched his hands as they smoothed soap over her leg. She loved the look of his immense hands moving tenderly to take care of her. It was as if she was the most important part of his life.

"Lie back to wet your hair," he instructed when he'd finished. Garrett pulled her scrunchie from her ponytail and helped her settle onto her back.

One hand supported her under her shoulders as she floated in the warm water. Her gaze jumped to his face as her Daddy lifted one leg from the water to drape over the side of the tub, spreading her thighs widely. Ellie watched his expression as he washed her intimately. The soft pouf glided through her pink folds, gently rasping over her tight bud before brushing between her bottom cheeks and her small sensitive opening.

"Daddy?"

"I'm glad you like my touch, Little girl," he reassured her as he set the ball of netting aside. "Hair next. Close your eyes."

Ellie squeezed her eyelids together as he brushed her hair through the water. Keeping them closed when he lifted her back into a seated position, Ellie heard the snap of a bottle top before feeling what had to be shampoo land on her hair. She treasured the luxurious feeling of being pampered as his fingers gently scrubbed the shampoo over her scalp and through her hair.

"Tilt your head back, Ellie," he requested.

After her Daddy rinsed the suds out by pouring fresh water from the spigot, he stood her on the mat, patted her dry, wrapped a towel around her, and reached for the blow dryer.

She watched in the mirror as he carefully combed out her hair and dried it. "I usually just go to bed with it damp," she informed him when he was finished.

"It's not good to sleep with a wet head, Rainbow." He swung her up in his arms and carried her from the bathroom, making her squeal.

When they entered the nursery, he kissed her forehead before settling her on the changing table and opening the towel.

She shivered, partly from the renewed exposure. It was one thing to sit in the tub and occupy herself with the crayons. She felt more exposed when lying on the changing table under his gaze.

Daddy pulled a strap across her tummy, trapping her hands at her sides.

She squirmed, the restraint turning her embarrassed exposure into arousal. "Daddy?"

He came to the end of the table and parted her legs, pushing them wide, knees bent. Then he gave a little tug to her curls. "I'm going to shave this off, Little one. I don't want your hands to get in the way."

She pursed her lips. He'd warned her this moment was coming, but now that it was here, she felt heat rush up her chest and over her cheeks. There wasn't much in life that could be more intimate than letting him shave her pussy. She would have no secrets from him after this. Including the fact that wetness was gathering between her folds.

Maybe he would think she was still damp from the bath.

She held her breath as he squeezed some shaving gel into his palm, rubbed his hands together to make a lather, and then spread it all over her mound.

"You can't hold your breath the entire time I shave you, Rainbow," he teased as he wiped his hands off and grabbed the razor. "I promise I'll be very careful. All you need to do is remain still. Can you do that for me?"

"Yes, Sir."

"Good girl." He set his fingers on her pelvis to steady her as he slowly dragged the razor through her curls.

Ellie squeezed her eyes shut so she didn't have to watch. She also tried to think of things that were icky to keep from reacting to this process. Muddy floors after a rain. Sticky chairs from children's fingers after eating one of her cupcakes. Spilled milk running across a table to drip onto the floor with a splash.

Nothing worked. As Daddy parted her folds and continued to shave between them, she grew more aroused. Her legs were trembling as he worked lower still, removing every hair all the way to her tight rear hole.

"There," he finally declared as he used a warm cloth to wipe away the shaving cream. "I'm proud of you, Rainbow. You held very still for Daddy."

Her breath hitched and her eyes popped open when he stroked his fingers over the smooth naked folds of her now denuded pussy.

He didn't stop. He wasn't just testing his work. He was intentionally fondling her now.

When she glanced down at him, he was watching her face. He slid his other hand from her pelvis to her breast, cupping the fullness of it before flicking his thumb over her nipple.

She arched her chest, gasping at the same time he pushed a finger up inside her tight pussy.

"So wet for me. I think my Little girl enjoys having Daddy shave her. I'm glad. You're so pretty with your pussy all smooth and bare for me."

She squirmed, panting now. "Daddy..."

"Look at Daddy, Rainbow. Tell me what you need."

She licked her suddenly very dry lips and met his gaze. "Will you have sex with me now, Daddy?" she asked, her voice barely above a whisper.

"Are you ready for that, Little one?"

She nodded, flushing deeper. "Please, Daddy."

He removed his fingers and brought them to his mouth, making her eyes widen as she watched him lick them languidly clean of her arousal. When he was done, he leaned over, kissed her lips, and nibbled a path to her breast, suckling one nipple and then the other.

As he lifted his face, he spoke again. "You're mine, Ellie. My Little girl. I know it in my soul. If I take you to my bed, I won't be able to let you go."

"I don't want you to let me go, Daddy." She didn't. Not ever. She wasn't sure she trusted that this amazing dream could really last and she would get to be Daddy's baby girl forever and ever, but she definitely wanted it to be true.

Daddy unfastened the strap across her middle to release her and then lifted her into his arms, cradling her against his chest. He carried her silently from the nursery to his bedroom and deposited her on the giant bed.

Shocking her, he tugged her hips to the edge, parted her legs with big hands on her thighs, and lowered his face to kiss her pussy.

She cried out at the unexpected sensation of his lips wrapping around her clit, his tongue flicking over the tip.

She wasn't a virgin. She'd had partners before, but no one had gone down on her like this. It was a new experience, one she found she really liked, and she fisted the covers at her sides as he thrust his tongue into her and then sucked again.

Already incredibly sensitive and aroused, it didn't take long for her to writhe in his grip, futilely bucking her hips against his palms as her orgasm slammed into her. "*Daddy*," she screamed as she came hard against his mouth.

He didn't stop. He kept milking her as she pulsed against his lips, the waves of pleasure slowly ebbing.

When he lifted his face to meet her gaze, he was grinning. "That must be what Rainbow tastes like. You said it was a flavor."

"Daddy," she admonished breathlessly.

She watched as he removed his clothes, teasing her with his lazy speed as if there were no hurry. She guessed there wasn't any reason to rush, but she wanted him inside her. *Now.*

It seemed like an eternity before he revealed the last part of him, his cock popping free of his boxers. It was large and made her mouth drop open. But he didn't give her much time to think about it before he grabbed a condom from the bedside table, rolled it onto his length, and climbed over her, scooting her across the bed at the same time.

He kissed her lips sweetly, angling his head to one side to deepen the contact after a few seconds.

She moaned into his mouth as she reached for him, wrapping her arms around his neck.

When the weight of him pressed against her, she parted her legs wider, loving the feel of his thick cock at her entrance.

Daddy finally broke free of her lips and met her gaze, his hands cupping her face. "You ready for this step, Rainbow?"

"Yes, Daddy," she murmured, squirming with need.

"It's a huge step, little one. I don't take it lightly."

"I know," she whispered, picking up on the seriousness in his tone. She didn't either. Not with him. She suspected he was going to claim more than just her body. After he took her fully, he would own her heart, too. Or perhaps he already did and this was just a formality.

Still cupping her face with one palm, he reached between them with his other hand, lined himself up with her entrance, and eased into her. He never released her gaze, even though her vision blurred and her jaw dropped open. "That's my girl," he praised. "Take all of Daddy."

She groaned as he punctuated his words by thrusting the rest of the way into her. Her body arched involuntarily, her hips lifting off the mattress to help him get deeper.

She slid her hands to his shoulders, her fingertips digging into his tight muscles as he eased out and thrust back in. When he did it again, she whimpered. Nothing had ever felt this good in her life. She'd never experienced this kind of connection with another human being. It was heaven. And she hoped she would be granted this experience ten hundred thousand billion times in the future.

Chapter Eleven

Garrett watched her face as she fell apart in his arms, humbled by how she responded to him, giving him everything he'd ever dreamed of and then some.

When her breath hitched right before she came, he gritted his teeth. He wanted to watch her come before he let himself follow. It was hard to hold back. His cock was about to explode. But he managed, not letting his own release consume him until she was sated and melting under him.

He groaned as he followed her over the edge, dropping his forehead to hers as the pulses of his orgasm sealed her to him forever. He hadn't been kidding earlier. If she changed her mind about being his forever Little girl now, he would be devastated.

"So precious," he whispered before he kissed her.

He didn't want to let her go, so he held her for a while before finally forcing himself to ease out of her and drop to one hip alongside her. He needed to go clean up and bring back a washcloth for her, too, but he didn't want this moment to end.

She smiled at him and cupped his face, her voice coming in a low, gravelly whisper. "I didn't know sex could be like that."

"Like what, Rainbow?" he questioned, unable to keep from grinning.

"So...special," she murmured.

He kissed her again. "It was special. I didn't know either, Little girl."

Her eyes widened. "You didn't?"

He shook his head. "Nope. I've never had a connection this strong with anyone." He hugged her closer to his side. "I want to pack up all your things and move you into my house. I want all our evenings to be spent like this. I want to take care of you in every way and never let you go."

She shuddered in his arms. He knew he was taking things at warp speed, but he also wanted to be sure she was aware of how serious he was.

"It's so soon, Daddy."

He kissed her again. "I know, Rainbow. And I won't rush you." He reluctantly let her go. "Be right back. Don't move."

He padded to the attached bathroom, disposed of the condom, cleaned up, and returned to her with a warm washcloth.

She blushed adorably as he spread her legs and wiped between them. When he was finished, he grabbed a diaper from the shelf under his bedside table and slid it under her cute bottom.

"You have diapers in the bedroom, Daddy?"

"Yep. Got to be able to get my girl covered back up and ready for bed." He shrugged into his jeans, lifted her into his arms, and carried her from the room. Part of him hated to put her to bed so soon, but she needed a new improved routine starting now.

He would prolong their time together with a story, but then it would be lights out for Ellie. "Would you like me to read you another chapter in our book?" he asked as he settled on the rocking chair, cradling her against him.

Her face lit up. "Yes, Daddy."

He grabbed a soft blanket from the arm of the chair and

wrapped it around her, tucking her in snuggly against his chest before he started to read.

After a few minutes, his phone vibrated in his back pocket. He ignored it and kept reading. This was his special time with Ellie. He didn't want any interruptions during her bedtime routine.

When her eyes grew heavy and she yawned, he glanced at the clock to see it was already seven-thirty.

He closed the book and set it aside. "Time for bed, Little girl."

She frowned. "It's so early, Daddy. I don't need to get up early tomorrow. Can't we start my bedtime in a few more days?"

He shook his head. "Nope. You need to start a new routine now. Otherwise, you'll be exhausted when the shop opens. I'm setting an alarm for three-thirty. I'll get you up and we'll go through the motions of your regular work schedule to help you acclimate."

She snuggled into him, wrapping her arms around his neck. "But I like sitting in your lap, Daddy."

"And I love having you in my lap, Rainbow." He patted her diaper-covered bottom. "I bet you were planning to work on more of your amazing cupcake creations tomorrow, weren't you?"

"Yes, but not until later in the day."

"Well, instead, you're going to start at four." He bopped her cute nose with his finger, loving the way she scrunched up her face and groaned.

"Would you like to go to bed with a sore bottom?"

She shook her head rapidly. "No, Sir."

His phone vibrated again as he rose and carried her to the crib. He settled her on her back, tucked the blanket around her, and slid Sprinkles and Cuddles into the crooks of her arms.

Ellie whispered introductions between the puppy and

unicorn. Of course, they were best friends immediately. Rewarding them, she hugged the stuffies close to her chest and kissed the top of the unicorn's head before repeating the care to Cuddles.

Garrett kissed her forehead and patted her tummy before lifting the side of the crib. "Remember, no climbing out of the crib. If you need Daddy, call out. I'll always have the other end of the monitor with me."

"Yes, Sir."

He headed for the window and pulled the new blackout curtains closed. He'd installed them earlier while she was interviewing.

She giggled from inside the crib. "Wow, that really blocks the light out."

"Yep. And wait until you see my next surprise." He flipped off the lights next to the door and strolled back toward her as she gasped.

"Daddy! There're stars on the ceiling. It's like nighttime in here." She giggled.

"That's the idea. I hope you like it."

"I love it. Now, I can pretend it's dark out and late at night."

"Sleep tight, Little girl. I'll wake you at three-thirty."

He stroked a stray hair from her forehead and had to force himself to leave the room. He would rather stay and watch her sleep, staring at her to keep reminding himself she was real. She was in his house. In his nursery. Sleeping in the crib.

He wanted her to be permanently his more than anything he'd ever wanted in his life.

He was smiling as he eased the door almost closed and headed for the living room, pulling out his phone. Two missed calls from Tarson Kirkwood, AKA Bear. Weird. The two of them knew each other from Blaze, but they didn't speak on the phone often.

Garrett grabbed the baby monitor and stepped out onto the back patio to return the call, not wanting to risk disturbing Ellie.

Tarson answered on the first ring. "Garrett. Thanks for calling me back."

"I didn't check to see if you'd left any messages. I just hit redial. What's up?"

"You know Daisy Galante, right?"

"Of course. She owns the florist shop in my building."

"Yes. Well, she had an incident this evening and she's pretty shook up."

Garrett stiffened. "What happened?" He didn't like hearing about any disturbances in his strip mall. This would make two in a week.

"Four guys came into her store as she was closing and harassed her."

"Shit," Garrett muttered under his breath, automatically assuming they must be the same four guys he'd seen bothering his Little. "Is she okay?"

"She's fine. Mostly they just wandered around in her store looking at everything and tossing their weight around. They asked her how much money she had in the cash register, but she'd already sent today's cash to the bank with her employee."

Garrett groaned. "Same thing happened to Ellie yesterday. I bet it's the same four thugs. I wonder if they're scoping out the area to plan which business would be worth robbing."

Tarson growled. "I don't like it."

"You and me both. I'm glad you'll be working with Ellie at Little Cakes. I don't like her being there alone."

"I agree. And that puts me close to the florist, too, but I can't be in both places at the same time."

Garrett rubbed his forehead. "I've hired some extra security to patrol the area. They start tomorrow. Did Daisy get any pictures by chance?"

"Even better. She has surveillance cameras."

"Good. I assume she called the police?"

"Yes. They've come and gone. They took the footage with them."

"Great. I'll call them in the morning and make sure they compare the footage with the pictures I took the other day. Maybe someone will recognize these thugs and we can get them off the street."

"Let's hope," Tarson agreed.

"Hey, how did you get involved?" Garrett asked, suddenly realizing he didn't know the connection.

"Daisy called me. We've known each other for years. She has my number in her phone. She knows I would have tanned her hide if she hadn't called me when she was in trouble like this."

Garrett chuckled. "I hear ya."

"I may spank her little bottom anyway just for being alone in the shop at closing time. That wasn't safe."

"I'm working on that with Ellie, too. These Little girls think they're invincible. I'm imagining it's going to take more than one solid spanking to get Ellie to see reason where her safety is concerned."

Tarson chuckled. "So, you and Ellie? Sounds like you're getting close."

"Yes. I hope so. She's a very special Little girl." Garrett glanced at the back door, smiling as he thought about his Little tucked in her crib in the nursery. He hoped she was his forever, but he wouldn't elaborate prematurely to Tarson.

He considered turning the conversation on Tarson and asking how close he was to Daisy, but decided against it. Not his business. Tarson had insinuated the two of them were friends. They both belonged to the same club. There was no reason to believe they had a relationship outside of the club.

Just because Tarson had said he would spank Daisy's bottom didn't mean he would do so in his home or hers. He might have been speaking of setting up a scene with her at Blaze to exact the disciplinary action.

"I'm happy for you, Garrett. Ellie's a sweet Little girl."

"Yes, she is. Thank you for calling. I'll stop by Daisy's shop tomorrow and touch base with her."

"I'll be around. I don't like the idea of four thugs harassing anyone on that strip. I'll pop in and out of the shops and keep an eye on things for the next few days before I start working at Little Cakes."

"Thank you. The extra set of eyes will be appreciated."

"No problem. Talk to you soon."

Garrett set the phone in his lap and tipped his head back toward the sky, smiling at the stars just beginning to show themselves. He loved that he'd created a nighttime environment for his Ellie. She'd seemed pleased. Hopefully, she would be able to sleep better and start a new routine that would be healthier for her.

Finally, he rose and went back inside. He needed to prep a smoothie for her to eat in the morning on the run, and then he needed to get to bed himself. If he was going to get Ellie up each morning at three-thirty, he would need to adjust his schedule and get to bed earlier, too.

It wouldn't be a hardship. He'd been a morning person for years. Early morning practices to avoid extreme heat had forced him to learn to get up before the crack of dawn when he'd played football. He'd never fully shaken the imbedded routine from his system.

Granted, three-thirty was earlier than he was used to, but for his Little he would make it his new schedule. After all, what was he going to do in the evenings after Ellie went to bed anyway?

After prepping for the morning smoothie, he turned out the lights in the kitchen and padded down the hall. He stopped to check on Ellie, pushing the door open a few inches and smiling as he listened to her snoring.

He could stand there all night and listen to her, but he eased the door almost closed again and headed for his own room. After he showered, Garrett remembered her suitcase. He tiptoed into her room with a stack of clothes and set them on top of the dresser. Putting them inside the drawers could wait until tomorrow.

Chapter Twelve

"Sleepy girl, it's time to wake up," a deep voice crooned next to her.

"Ten minutes more," she pleaded, turning over to face the wall.

"It's time to get up, Little girl. You slept well in your crib last night. Think of all the cupcakes waiting for you at the bakery."

"I love cupcakes," she mumbled.

"I love your cupcakes, too. Could you make one for me without frosting?" he asked, tugging the blanket from her warm body.

Ellie whirled around to look at him incredulously. Instantly, she was completely awake. "You don't like frosting?"

"I like the cake better," he confessed.

"Cake is good," she allowed as she sat up and cooperated as he lifted her to the ground. "But there has to be a law somewhere that cupcakes have to be frosted."

"Potty," he instructed, helping her with a firm squeeze, compressing her tummy and lower back toward her core.

A faint hiss in her diaper had Ellie talking to cover the revealing sound. "You'd really like a naked cupcake?"

"Yes. I like the sound of that. Maybe you should sell those, too. Maybe they would appeal to health-conscious customers," Garrett suggested as he led her to the changing table.

Contemplating that possibility, Ellie laid still as her Daddy changed her diaper and helped her hop down to stand. Feeling the air, she brushed her hand over her bare bottom. "Don't I need a diaper?"

"Panties to go to work, Little girl. Diaper at home."

Ellie almost felt sad as her Daddy helped her step into her regular cotton panties and leggings. As he fastened her bra, she looked over her shoulder. "Did you unpack for me?" she asked.

"I did. Is this one okay?" he asked, holding up a bright blue T-shirt.

"Sure." Ellie held her arms up so he could drop it over her and smooth the material into place.

She held still as Garrett brushed her hair and gathered it into a high ponytail that would stay out of the way as she worked. Ellie loved his care. It made her feel cherished and special. Tears gathered in her eyes. When he turned her around, they rolled down her cheeks.

"Oh, Little girl. Why are you crying?" he probed quietly.

"I don't know!" she answered, scrubbing her hands over her face.

"Do you like Daddy taking care of you?"

"I love it," she whispered.

"So much it makes you cry happy tears?"

"Yes." Her voice warbled with emotion.

Her Daddy pulled her tightly against him and hugged her fiercely. "You're mine, Little girl. I'll never let you go."

"Never?"

"Never." Garrett eased her back from his body and captured her lips.

His kiss was demanding. Ellie clung to him, grabbing hand-fuls of his shirt to stabilize herself. Her Daddy would not allow her to be partially connected to him. Garrett wanted everything from her.

When he lifted his lips from hers, Ellie nodded. She wasn't sure what she was agreeing with exactly, but his devasting smile made her feel even warmer inside. Allowing him to guide her through the house and out to his SUV, Ellie clung to his hand, needing to be close to him. She dutifully sipped the smoothie that her Daddy pressed into her hands when he tucked her safely into the vehicle.

They were both quiet on the drive to her shop, each lost in their own thoughts but holding hands to stay in contact with the other. Too soon, Garrett parked at the front of the shop and exited to help her out. He unlocked Little Cakes and swept through the bakery to make sure all was well.

"Alright, Little girl. We're here right on time. You're ready to get your day started. Call or text me if you need me."

"Can I contact you just to chat?" she hesitantly asked.

"I'd love that."

Her Daddy swept her into his arms and hugged her close. "I'll see you this afternoon. Lock the door behind me," he instructed.

"Yes, Daddy," she answered automatically before lifting her lips to invite his kiss.

"Good girl."

She was still thinking about that fiery kiss as she turned to walk into the kitchen. A loud rapping on the door made her turn to see Garrett pointing at the lock.

"Oops!" Ellie ran over to flip the lever to secure the door. She laughed at his waggling finger reprimanding her.

"Be good," he called through the door before heading back to his SUV.

She waved happily through the window until he drove out of sight. Hugging her arms around her torso, Ellie headed for the kitchen. There were so many cupcakes to get ready for the grand opening!

Once the sun was up, Ellie opened the front door so her staff could enter for training. She knew Garrett wanted her locked inside but it just wasn't practical with all the deliveries and training. Working hard on the decorations and setting up the displays in the cases while batches of cupcakes rose in the oven, Ellie kept an eye on the traffic outside.

Tori was the first to come through the door, and Ellie beamed as she entered. "Hi, Tori! I'm glad you're here for the training. You're the first to arrive. Let me show you how to clock in."

Ellie showed her where the time clock hung in the back supply room. Plucking a colorful nametag from the rack, she handed it to the woman in her thirties.

"Here you go. You'll need this badge every day. This will clip onto your Little Cakes apron. You can wear a colored T-shirt and jeans or shorts depending on the season. Nothing too revealing—like holes in private places. You should look casual but not like you're hanging at a club or at home. Make sure you wear sneakers that cover your entire foot. The health department here requires that. No flipflops or sandals."

"Got it. T-shirt, jeans, and tennis shoes. I can do that."

"You'll use your ID to log in. You try it. Wave it across the sensor," Ellie directed. She smiled at the mechanical beep that signaled the machine worked perfectly.

"Let's get you an apron."

Ellie opened a cabinet next to the time clock. "You can get a fresh apron here each day and leave your old one in that bin when you log out," she explained, pointing to the large bin.

"Awesome. I love this design. Did you create it?" Tori asked, pointing to the store's embroidered logo on the front.

"Goodness no. I don't have a creative bone in my body. I hired a designer. How I'm going to make a special board look legible, I don't know," Ellie confessed.

"I'm pretty artistic. I'd love to try!"

"Yay! I've got everything set out. Let's see what you come up with."

Soon, Tori was entrenched in creating a beautiful announcement using the neon markers on Ellie's blackboard. Amazed at the swirls and decorations her new employee crafted around the featured cupcake, Ellie knew she'd found the right person for that job.

Things were just falling into place. Ellie couldn't wait for the grand opening. She knew her dream of running Little Cakes would be a success. Ellie didn't want to derail her success by missing an important component, so she forced herself to concentrate on training her employees. Carefully, she checked off all the items on her list.

Several people popped their heads in to say hello and ask when she'd be open. Ellie was tickled that they were eager to try her goodies when they passed the front door while shopping. She handed out a lot of flyers advertising the grand opening specials to encourage everyone to come back.

The day flew past with the window display artists coming to paint her logo and business hours on the windows and doors. Ellie loved that everything was coming together so well. The store was just as she had envisioned.

By the end of the day, Ellie was exhausted. She waved goodbye to Tori, Sue, and Riley. Lark received a hug for stopping by during some free time to learn how to use the cash register.

"Thank you so much," Ellie said as she stepped away from her friend.

"It's so much fun here. People are going to flock here in droves," Lark assured her. "You know what realtors always say..."

The two women recited together, "Location. Location. Location."

Giggling at their silliness, the two friends turned to look out the front windows. All day long, everyone who walked past the window had stopped and pointed to the logo on the door. Just at that moment, a young boy cupped his hands around his eyes to peer inside. Ellie and Lark waved and pointed to a sign that announced the countdown. He grinned and turned to share the information with his mom.

Ellie crossed her fingers behind her back. *Please, please, let Little Cakes be a huge success!*

Chapter Thirteen

Bear lifted a cooled batch of cupcakes and carried them to the decorating table. These would be the first round of the new treats he had envisioned. The small, premium chocolate logos announcing Little Cakes were ready to go. He couldn't wait to see all the pieces come together.

Glancing at the tense Little girl working nearby, he knew she was stressed. He'd let Garrett know she needed some tender loving care that night or she'd never unwind. They worked well together. They'd spent two days making sure there were enough cupcakes for practically the entire town, and the display shelves were almost full.

"Do you think we'll have enough cupcakes for tomorrow?" Ellie asked. Her front teeth worried her bottom lip.

"If you sell all these cupcakes tomorrow, I'll bake all night to stock you up for the next day. It's going to be okay, Ellie. Don't panic if you run out of some flavors. People will buy a different flavor and fall in love with that one."

"The girls are putting together boxes for one, two, a half-dozen, and a dozen cupcakes. I hope I have enough."

"You're looking at this all wrong, Little girl. You want to sell out of everything. We can scramble and get more containers.

You've already planned for more cupcakes than could fill the bakery even if they were stacked on top of each other."

"I know I'm worrying. I want everything to go perfectly tomorrow," Ellie said, applying a thin coat of frosting to a few cupcakes in that batch.

"Something will go wrong and that's okay. You'll compensate for it and learn."

He skillfully changed the subject to distract her. "Who came up with the idea for naked cupcakes? You'll pull all the diet conscious people in with that."

"Daddy," Ellie said.

Bear counted slowly, waiting for her to realize what she had just admitted.

"Oh! I mean Garrett," she said in a rush.

Bear loved the pink blush that covered her cheeks. "You can claim him, Ellie. I know he's sure you're his, too."

"How does he know so fast?" Ellie whispered.

"What does your heart say?"

"It says he's my Daddy and I love him."

"I think Garrett is listening to his feelings as well," Bear confided. "Smart Daddies always do."

The buzz of the timer on the oven interrupted their conversation. Ellie scrambled to turn it off and lift the last batch of cupcakes to the cooling rack. When she returned, Bear was pleased to see Ellie smiling as she decorated the naked cakes. Maybe he'd helped the Little girl fret about one less thing.

He couldn't keep from grinning as her tongue darted out in concentration. His heart warmed. Garrett was a lucky man to have found his perfect Little. Bear hoped one day he would be so lucky. He knew the exact right Little was out there for him.

Garrett pulled into a space in front of Little Cakes. He strolled in to find the three new counter workers stacking to go cupcake boxes against the wall. By the look of the pile of containers and the delicious smell of the cupcakes, he knew they'd all worked hard to prepare for tomorrow.

"Hi, Ladies. I'm Garrett," he introduced himself. Of the three women, he only knew Riley.

"Hi, Garrett. Ellie told us you might stop by some time." Riley nodded toward the other two women. "That's Tori and Sue. Ellie's in the back with Bear."

"D... Garrett!" Ellie burst through the swinging door to greet him.

"Hi, sweetheart! You've been busy!"

"We have naked cupcakes," she announced proudly, tugging him over to the display counter.

"Do I have to wait until tomorrow to eat one?" he asked, wrapping one arm around her to hug his Little girl to his side.

"No. I'd love to hear your reaction. What flavor would you like?"

"How about good old chocolate?"

Ellie opened the case and selected a lightly frosted cupcake. Handing it to him with a flourish, she watched him eagerly to judge his reaction to the treat.

Carefully, Garrett examined it from all sides. "Looks like the perfect ratio of frosting to cake."

Pulling the paper liner from around the moist cake, Garrett inhaled the deep chocolate aroma. He lifted the cupcake to his mouth and took a large bite. Rich flavor captivated his tastebuds. An honest moan of delight sprang from him. Ellie bounced up and down in front of him at his obvious approval.

Garrett swallowed and held up one finger to make her wait as he took another bite. "You have ruined me for any other dessert. This is scrumptious!"

"Just wait until you try some of the fancy flavors," she told him. "Look at the board Tori created for me! It will tell the special cupcake of the week."

"Rainbow Sprinkles," he read, feeling his lips curve with delight. "That's perfect!"

"Are you all open?" an excited voice came from the doorway.

Ellie turned with a big smile to answer the eager customer. "Tomorrow is the grand opening. Would you like a coupon to bring back?" she asked, picking up a flyer and walking forward.

"My pregnant wife might let me back in the car if I come back with that," the man laughed. "Oh, look. The list of cupcakes is on the back. That will help her wait until tomorrow. She'll plot which ones we need to try."

"Oh, you'll need to try them all," Riley suggested.

"Don't I know it. I'm not going to tell her how good it smells in here. I'll just escort her in tomorrow." He waved goodbye as he headed back to the car idling at to the curb.

"You may need to create a frequent flyer program for your future addicts," Garrett suggested.

"She's already got that covered. Ellie is a marketing genius," Bear's deep voice observed as he walked through the swinging door.

"Thanks, Bear. Go home and sleep. Thank you for your help today to get ready," Ellie said with a smile.

"If you run out of cupcakes tomorrow and need me to come in after you close, send me a text. I can always come in and get some batches into the oven."

Garrett followed the large man out of the bakery after Bear had said goodbye to all the ladies. "How's Daisy?"

"She's okay now that it's daylight. I know she's not going to want to be alone in her shop for a while. Do you have any leads on the four men?" Bear asked.

"No. A few sightings every few days but nothing consistent that the police have been able to follow up on. I don't like this. Not only as the owner of the commercial real estate but as Ellie's Daddy. I don't want to think of anything that might be dangerous coming close to her."

"I'm sure they'll be caught soon. They can't keep evading everyone for too long," Bear observed.

"I hope so."

"You all coming to Blaze tonight?"

"Not tonight. Ellie needs to be in bed early tonight."

"Good luck with that. She's exhausted but she's eaten cupcakes all day. Her body is one sugar molecule away from an explosion," Bear warned.

"I need to get some good nutrition into her. Thanks for cluing me in." Garrett waved as the Little Cakes' employees emerged from the shop to head home for the night. "I'd better get in there before she comes up with an even better idea for a cupcake."

Leaving Bear laughing, Garrett jogged back to the door. He flipped the lock from inside and walked through the dining area to the kitchen. "Nope. Put that butter back in the refrigerator."

"But I need to make one more batch of Rainbow Sprinkles for tomorrow," Ellie protested, holding the industrial blocks wrapped in wax paper to her apron.

"In the refrigerator, Little girl. You have lots of cupcakes."

She leaned forward to whisper confidentially, "There can never be too many cupcakes."

Garrett arched one eyebrow and crossed his arms in front of his chest. They were at an impasse. He knew she needed to leave for the day. No more cupcakes would be created in that kitchen that evening.

"What are you going to do? Spank me?" she challenged.

"If I need to," he answered evenly.

Ellie tried to dart around him to the large mixer, but Garrett had wrangled too many tight ends during his time in football. Within seconds, he had her controlled at his side, dangling from his arm wrapped around her waist. Carrying her easily to the large walk-in cooler that housed the prepared cupcakes, Garrett opened the door and entered.

"How many cupcakes do you calculate are in here?" he asked.

"One, two, three..." Ellie began counting racks of cupcakes.

When she slowed down, Garrett lifted her to shoulder height so she could count the racks Bear had obviously placed up high.

With an "oh!" Ellie continued to count.

Garrett interrupted her a few seconds later as she attempted the higher math to multiply the number of racks by two dozen. "You have almost enough cupcakes for half of the city to stop by tomorrow."

"What if..."

He held a hand up to interrupt Ellie. "Some are babies with no teeth and adults who don't like sweets."

Her gasp of protest that anyone wouldn't like her cupcakes made him struggle to control the smile that threatened to appear on his face. "Weird people exist, Rainbow."

Walking out of the cooler, he carried her back to the supply fridge and opened the door. "Put the butter back."

Reluctantly, she reached out to place the industrial-sized blocks onto the shelf.

"Good girl." Garrett carried her away from the baking area. He wasn't going to set her feet back down on the floor until she was as far away as possible. Hooking one finger through the loops on her jeans, Garrett made sure she would stay by him as he pulled the apron over her head.

"Home, Little girl," he announced after tossing the well spattered garment into the used bin.

"I can come in early tomorrow, right?"

"Yes. I'll wake you up to be here before the sun comes up."

Wrapping his arm around her, Garrett walked Ellie to the door and locked up after them. He settled her into the SUV and got in quickly to drive home carefully. "Dinner, bath, and bed."

"I'm not hungry."

"I bet you'll be tempted by my mashed potato soup," Garrett suggested.

"I've never had mashed potato soup," Ellie commented, turning sideways in her seat to look at him.

"I think you'll like it a lot. It's one of my specialties."

"Yum. I like potato soup with cheese on top. Is that how you serve it?"

"You'll see. I devised a special concoction for my Little girl."

"Just for me?"

"Only for you, Rainbow."

As Garrett turned a corner, Ellie reached a hand across the console dividing the front seats. Garrett linked his fingers with hers and raised the back of her hand to his mouth. After pressing a warm kiss to her skin, he rested their hands on his thigh. Her small sound of contentment went straight to his heart.

Chapter Fourteen

Ellie relaxed against the soft leather seat. She hadn't realized how tired she was until they were on their way home. Startled, her mind focused on that word. Home. Did she already feel like Garrett's home was hers?

Peeking over at him, Ellie studied his profile. Garrett maneuvered the vehicle through traffic. It didn't feel like she'd just met him a few days ago. She felt better being with him. Even when she was so focused at work, the thought of him had drifted through her mind and Ellie had found herself smiling. Was this what having a Daddy felt like?

"You're thinking awfully hard over there, Little girl. Anything you want to tell Daddy?"

"I missed you today," she answered simply. That seemed to sum up all her feelings.

"I missed you today, too, Rainbow."

Garrett drove into the driveway and let go of her hand to trigger the garage door opener on his visor. Ellie sat patiently as he parked the car and came around to help her out. Once standing, she wrapped her arms around his waist and hugged her Daddy tight.

He kissed her tenderly before running the tip of his tongue

up the curve of her neck. "Mmm! Sweet. Shower first, sugar girl."

Leading her into the house filled with the aroma of soup, Garrett stopped at the washing machine. "I think you bathed in your ingredients, Little girl. Clothes in the washer."

Before she processed his words, her Daddy lifted her T-shirt over her head and dropped it in the washer. A fine cloud of floury sugar puffed into the air, making her laugh. As he unfastened her jeans, Ellie laughed again. "I did actually get most of the ingredients into the mixing bowl."

"I saw all the cupcakes. I think you're wearing at least two now," Garrett remarked, kneeling at her feet to slip off her shoes and tug the jeans from her body. Tossing those into the washer as well, he leaned forward to swirl his tongue over her belly button. "Mmm! Do you taste so sweet everywhere?"

Nodding yes, Ellie held her breath as the heat level in the small room intensified. She squeezed her thighs together, feeling herself become wet as her body and mind responded to him. Slowly, he lowered her panties until they looped around her ankles.

"Step," he commanded. As she obeyed, he removed the lacy garment and swept her socks from her feet.

Garrett's hands slowly eased up the outer sides of her legs from ankle to hips. Ellie watched him lean forward slowly until his nose brushed her sensitive, bare mound. His deep inhale made her breathe with him. The intimacy of him scenting her fueled the heat building deep inside her.

"Daddy!" she whispered urgently.

His tongue traced the seam of her pussy lightly. Ellie leaned back against the appliances behind her for stability as her legs became unsteady. Repeating his intimate path, Garrett pressed his tongue into her pink folds, his hum of pleasure vibrating against her. She grabbed his shoulders, trying to steady herself as his intimate caresses continued.

"Oh!" she gasped when Garrett wrapped his arms around

her hips, lifting her as he rose to his feet. Her powerful Daddy easily handled her weight as if she were truly little.

Ellie shivered as he sat her on the cool metal of the dryer.

"Open," he ordered, pressing her knees apart.

Frozen, she watched him looking at her. The most private parts of her were on display as he devoured her with his gaze. With a visible jerk, Garrett tore himself away from studying her. His green eyes, darkened by passion, linked with hers.

"Mine!"

She nodded without hesitation, submitting to his claim. Garrett rewarded her with a hard kiss that made her toes curl with the thrill of his mastery. His hands swept away her last garment, flinging the lacy bra into the washer. He trailed blazing kisses down her throat and over her collarbone as his palms caressed her full breasts.

"Ah!" she gasped when he pinched one nipple before soothing it with rough brushes of his thumb. Ellie waited for him to repeat the tinge of pain to the other, holding her breath in anticipation. Her hands traced over his broad shoulders, clinging to his powerful muscles as he tasted her skin on his descending path.

His mouth captured the neglected nipple. Sucking it deep into his warmth, Garrett brushed his tongue across the beaded tip, making it harden even further. As he released the draw on her breast, Garrett captured the peak between his teeth. Ellie moaned in delight as he nipped it before soothing the sting with a stroke of his tongue.

"Daddy! Please," she whispered. She wiggled on the metal, feeling her slick juices on the hard surface. Ellie had never wanted anyone more.

"Shh, Little girl. Daddy will make it better."

Garrett drew a finger over her rounded tummy. Ellie sucked in her stomach, trying to make it disappear. Tilting his face up to look at her, Garrett shook his head. In a low, growling voice, he admonished her, "You are perfect just as you are. Never try to change to please me."

Ellie nodded and lifted one hand from his shoulder to trace an X on her chest. "Cross my heart," she promised.

"Good girl. Now, lean back."

Following his directions, Ellie pressed her shoulders against the wall. She watched him kneel in front of the dryer.

Garrett wrapped his immense hands around her thighs and pulled her forward.

"Oh!" she cried, off-balance as she slid on the metal surface. Her hands covered his.

Garrett held her in place as he lowered his mouth. Unable to tear her eyes away from the erotic display of his lips and tongue tasting her, Ellie froze as pleasure buffeted her body. Her hands remained glued to her thighs when he tugged his fingers from under hers to touch her. After tracing her opening with his index finger, Garrett pressed two fingers deep into her body.

"Yes!" she moaned as his lips sealed around that sensitive bud. Her hips bucked up against his mouth as he drew on her clit. Ellie couldn't resist the combination of the thrusts of his fingers and the feel of his tongue tantalizing that sensitive cluster of nerves. Pleasure flooded her body as she orgasmed hard.

She didn't move as Garrett stood and gathered her limp body against him. He carried her to his bedroom, stopping to pull a small packet from the nightstand. Garrett walked into the master bathroom to the massive, walk-in shower. He set her feet down on the ground and held her securely to his side as he adjusted the water.

"Hold on to the wall, Little girl," he directed. The moment she could stand on her own, he undressed and threw his clothes into the corner of the bathroom. Rejoining her, Garrett moved the showerhead to cascade over their bodies.

Ellie continued watching over her shoulder and saw him rip open the condom and sheathe himself with it. His shaft, thick and eager, soon pressed against her as Garrett aligned their bodies.

"This is going to be fast, Little girl. Hold on!" he warned before filling her completely in one quick thrust that pushed the breath from her lungs.

Ellie flattened her hands on the cold tile and pressed her bottom toward him, offering herself to his thrusts. Her mind and body responded eagerly to his possession. She craved his touch.

One of his hands roamed over her body as he loomed behind Ellie. His other arm wrapped around her abdomen, holding her in place. Over and over, he thrust into her tight passage until their breaths were ragged and uneven. That caressing hand moved between her thighs and Ellie pressed her forehead against the tile, trying to hold off her approaching orgasm.

"Now, Little girl," he commanded, tweaking her clit and launching Ellie into another massive orgasm. Her spasming passage spurred his pleasure and Garrett's shout of completion echoed in the tiled enclosure.

The warm water pounded down on their skin as they recovered. When Garrett shifted to withdraw from her body, Ellie turned to press herself fully against him. She snuggled her head in the crook of his neck. His arms wrapped around her to hold her close.

"Little girl, I love you," he said huskily against her hair.

Ellie pulled away slightly to meet his gaze. "You love me?" she repeated.

His lips curved in an indulgent smile. "You're my Little. I love you with all my heart."

When she opened her mouth to let him know how she felt as well, Garrett placed a finger over her lips. "Tell me when you're sure, Ellie. I know you care for me."

She nodded, unsure whether she was agreeing with his directions or his assessment of her feelings. Thrilled by his careful handling of her feelings, Ellie's heart swelled in her chest. He didn't want her to just parrot the words back. He wanted all of her.

Quickly, Garrett washed their bodies, then wrapped Ellie in a soft towel before drying himself off. Leading her out of the shower, he stopped to step into a pair of shorts.

"Let's get some food in your tummy."

"Mashed potato soup?" she reminded him. The delicious aroma beckoned from the kitchen.

"Yes, Rainbow. Soup for my baby."

Following him into the kitchen, Ellie watched him fill a thick-walled bottle with the rich soup and screw a lid with a nipple on top. "I'm going to drink from that?" she asked.

"Come sit on Daddy's lap." Garrett led her to the leather couch and sat down. He helped her sit on his lap and recline back in his arms against the pillows. Wiggling the nipple into her mouth, he held the bottle steady as she sucked experimentally.

It was so good! Ellie pulled strongly on the large nipple. It felt strange in her mouth, but the soup was so good, she couldn't resist drinking more. She wiggled into a comfortable position and relaxed. Her eyes closed as she finished the soup. Hard work, pleasure, and a warm, full tummy combined to make her sleepy.

Garrett set the bottle aside when she finished. Rising easily to his feet with her cradled in his arms, Ellie melted against him as he carried her through the house. He eased the towel from around her and sat her on the vanity. She leaned against his chest with her eyes closed.

"Open your mouth, Rainbow. Let Daddy brush your teeth before I tuck you into bed."

Obediently, she opened her mouth. Fresh minty toothpaste erased the thick, delicious soup. It felt weird having someone else brush her teeth, but she liked it. *He takes such good care of me.*

After she rinsed her mouth, Garrett asked quietly, "Potty or diaper?"

"Diaper," she whispered.

Within minutes, Ellie was wrapped in a thick protector and snuggled under her covers with Sprinkles and Cuddles hugged close. Closing her eyes, she was almost asleep when she felt Garrett's lips press a kiss to her forehead.

"Love you, Daddy," she whispered before tumbling into oblivion.

Chapter Fifteen

The scent of bacon yanked Ellie from sleep. It took her one second of glancing around to realize where she was, another second to acknowledge that her Daddy was making her breakfast, and a third second to bolt to sitting as she remembered today was opening day for Little Cakes.

"Daddy!" she squealed as she rose onto her knees and gripped the railing of her crib. She wasn't sure what time it might be, but she knew Garrett would never let her oversleep on her opening day. She was so anxious though that her heart raced as she waited for him to enter the nursery.

He was beaming, his smile so wide that she clapped her hands together. "I guess you smelled the bacon."

"Yes, Daddy. Are you making me breakfast?"

"I sure am," he stated as he lowered the side of the crib and lifted her into his arms. He swung her around in a full circle before settling her on her back on the changing table.

She started giggling, filled with both excitement and nerves. She couldn't lie still even when Daddy settled her arms at her sides and secured her to the table with a strap.

"Someone's filled with anxious energy this morning," he teased as he flattened his big hand on her tummy.

She wiggled under his touch. "Do you think people will come? What if no one comes?" She worried her bottom lip with her teeth.

He chuckled as he rounded to the end of the table to remove her diaper. "Half the town will be there before noon, Rainbow. I'm sure of it. Don't you worry."

"But what if they don't?" She'd had nightmares for weeks. Each of them was the same: she flipped the sign to OPEN, unlocked the door, and no one came in. She always woke up panting.

Surprisingly, she hadn't had that bad dream since meeting Daddy. Maybe she'd been extra tired lately or maybe he had a way of calming her that helped her rest better. It was probably a combination of both those facts in addition to the amazing orgasms he gave her.

She flushed at the memory of him setting her on the dryer, holding her thighs wide, and thrusting his tongue into her last night.

"I promise they will, Little one," Daddy said as he removed her diaper, glancing up at her and then freezing. A slow smile spread across his face. "What's going through that mind of yours, Rainbow? The flush on your face can't possibly be caused by your trepidation about opening day." He tapped her pussy with his fingers.

Even more heat rose up her chest and cheeks as she pursed her lips. No way could she tell him she'd been distracted by memories of his mouth on her down *there*.

Daddy spread her legs farther and parted her lower lips before dragging a finger through her folds and circling her clit.

Ellie moaned as she tipped her head back and arched her chest. "Daddy..."

"Perhaps the best way to start your big day is with an orgasm. Lucky for you, we have plenty of time. Though I don't think you'll need more than a minute." He thrust two fingers into her to punctuate his words.

Ellie cried out, instinctively drawing her knees together.

"Uh uh, Little one. Keep your legs parted for me."

She trembled as she spread her thighs wider, whimpering because he was teasing her clit with one finger, tapping it slowly. She needed more. More pressure. More something.

Daddy didn't let her down. He added a finger, thrusting three into her now while he slid his other hand to her pelvis to hold her steady. His thumb came to her clit, pressing against it and rubbing.

She was so wet and aroused that it only took a few seconds to reach her release. Her entire body shuddered as she came hard around his fingers, crying out at the same time.

Daddy's voice was deep when he murmured, "You're so precious, Rainbow. I'll never tire of watching you come." He placed a chaste kiss on her pussy before wiping her arousal away with a wet wipe.

Moments later, she was unfastened and on her feet. Daddy had set out clothes for her, and she giggled when she noticed the boldly colored shirt on top. She clapped her hands together. "Where did you find that, Daddy?" The shirt was vertically striped with every color of the rainbow on it.

"Found it online and ordered it for you. Do you like it?"

"I love it," she declared as he helped her into her bra and then held the shirt over her head.

"Arms up."

The cotton material was soft and it fit her perfectly. Still naked from the waist down, she threw her arms around his neck and hugged him tight. "Thank you, Daddy."

He was grinning as he eased her back and held up a pair of panties next.

She laughed. "Daddy! Those are even better." She snagged them from his hands to examine the brightly colored cupcakes scattered all over the panties.

"No one but me will know you're wearing them, but I

wanted you to feel special on your big day." He tugged them from her fingers and bent down. "Step in."

She was grinning from ear to ear as he helped her into her jeans next and then her shoes and socks.

After a trip to the bathroom to brush her teeth and pull her hair up into a high ponytail, he kissed the tip of her nose. "Breakfast first and then we can get to the shop. It's still early, but I know you'll be restless if I don't get you there hours ahead of schedule."

He was right. She was jittery. She skipped down the hallway and climbed on to her highchair in the kitchen, fighting against the butterflies in her tummy. "I'm not sure I can eat, Daddy."

He turned toward her from the stove and gave her a stern look. "You can't go to work on your first day without a nutritious breakfast, Rainbow. Daddy's orders."

She sighed and lowered her shoulders. "Yes, Sir." She wasn't sure how she could swallow even one bite even though the bacon smelled amazing. All she could think about every time she caught a whiff was that she really needed to come up with a cupcake that had bacon crumbles on the top soon. Maybe a pancake cupcake with maple syrup frosting and bacon. Yes!

"I can see your mind working over there, Little one." Daddy chuckled. "How many cupcakes have you designed in your mind so far this morning?"

She grinned. "Just the one."

"I can't wait to try it." He slid a plate of bacon, eggs, and toast in front of her before adding a cup of orange juice with a lid. "I didn't give you more than you can handle," he said, giving her a stern look. "I expect you to clean your plate."

"Yes, Sir." She sighed as she picked up her fork. The first bite was hard to chew and swallow, but then she realized she was actually hungry and polished it all off in no time.

"Good girl." Daddy was eating next to her, his plate piled much higher than hers. He finished at the same time.

"Can we go now, Daddy?" She swung her legs.

"After I finish my coffee."

"We can make you more coffee at the shop," she told him, hoping he would take her up on that offer.

He chuckled as he leaned over and bopped her nose. "There's plenty of time, Rainbow. The store doesn't open for hours."

"I know, but I'm anxious." She couldn't sit still, and it was a struggle to wait patiently, but she didn't badger her Daddy again.

Before she knew it, they were out the door and heading for the SUV.

Chapter Sixteen

"Ready?" Garrett shouted from his place by the front door. He had his hand on the sign, ready to flip it over and unlock the door. His gaze shifted around the room.

Ellie stood near him, wringing her hands nervously.

Lark was at the cash register. Tori was next to Lark, ready to fill orders. Sue was in the middle of the room, prepared to hand out today's menu and help customers understand where to line up. Riley was in the back, ready to bring out more cupcakes as they were needed.

Ellie nodded. "Let's do it." She was excited about the line that had slowly grown outside as people waited for the shop to open. She couldn't tell how far it extended, but long enough that she could no longer see the end. She thought it wrapped around the corner.

The line was a good sign, but it also intimidated her. What if they couldn't keep up with so many patrons all at once on opening day?

"Little Cakes is officially open for business," Daddy declared as he opened the front door.

Ellie smiled so broadly that her face hurt as the noisy crowd filled her store. She was beyond grateful for every single one of the women she'd hired because they proved to be efficient and worked well together under the stress of the grand opening.

Within minutes, a line had formed at the cash register, and Lark was ringing people out while Tori handed them their selections.

Ellie spent most of her time working the crowd, introducing herself to everyone she could, making sure they had napkins and forks and water cups if they hadn't bought a drink.

Within a half an hour, every table was filled and people were spilling out onto the sidewalk with their cupcakes. Based on the moans of delight every time someone took their first bite, Ellie was giddy with excitement.

Two hands curled on her shoulders from behind, and Ellie tipped her head back to smile at Daddy. He kissed the top of her head. "They love it," he murmured.

She believed him. The proof was on their wide-eyed, smiling faces. "I should go check on Riley in the back and see if we're running out of anything."

He gave her shoulders a squeeze. "Okay, but don't panic if you are. That's a good thing. You'll learn which cupcakes are a favorite and make more of them in the future. You can't provide an infinite supply of every flavor every day. Don't beat yourself up if something runs out." He lifted a brow.

She nodded. She knew he was right, but she still wanted to have as many of each variety as possible.

The next several hours went by so quickly that Ellie was shocked when she noticed it was after three. She grumbled when Garrett leaned over to whisper in her ear. "Time to break for something to eat, Little girl."

His voice was no nonsense, but she still protested, twisting around to look at him. "I can't leave the floor on opening day. What if someone needs me?"

He tipped her chin back with one hand and leaned in so that his lips were close to her ear. "You have to eat, Rainbow. It's already way past lunchtime. I know you don't want me to take you to the back room and spank your bottom with all these people in the shop."

She shivered at his suggestion. "You wouldn't."

"You want to test that theory?" He leaned back, eyebrows high.

She swallowed. He looked serious. "Okay, fine."

"Good girl. I made you a sandwich before you got up this morning. I bet you didn't even notice I brought lunch with us."

She shook her head. She hadn't noticed much of anything. She'd been too excited.

As Daddy took her hand and led her to the back room, she turned her head toward the cash register. "I'll be back in ten."

"No worries," Lark responded. "Everyone's had a lunch break but you. Go eat something before you faint." She grinned. Ellie truly had the best friends ever.

As soon as they entered the back room, Daddy pointed toward a stool at the counter. "Sit." He headed into the cooler and returned with a brown paper bag from which he removed three sandwiches, a baggie of apple wedges, and two bottles of water.

Ellie stared at him as he unwrapped her sandwich and set it in front of her. "Ham and swiss. Whole wheat bread, but I did cut off the crusts."

Her chest tightened. She didn't even glance down at the sandwich as she stared at him. How did he know her so well after such a short time? And how had she gotten so lucky to have found a Daddy who took such good care of her?

"What?" he asked, a lopsided grin spreading across his face.

"I love you."

His eyes widened and then his smile grew. "I know. You told me last night."

"Yeah, but I was almost asleep at the time. You might have thought I was being flippant. I mean it." She glanced around to make sure they were alone. "I love you, Daddy."

He leaned closer to her, cupped the back of her head, and

kissed her soundly. "I love you too, Rainbow. I'm the luckiest man in the world."

She couldn't stop smiling as he leaned back and pointed at her sandwich again. "Eat, Little one. You need sustenance. More than just sugar."

She picked up the first triangle and devoured it. She really was hungry. It had been hours since he'd fed her breakfast. It was hard not to scarf her food down. She kept glancing at the door that led to the front, but she forced herself to eat at a reasonable pace.

Ellie had just swallowed the last bite of sandwich and was crunching on an apple slice when a commotion out front made her back stiffen.

Daddy jumped to his feet at the sound of loud, angry, male voices, turning and rushing back toward the front before Ellie could even slide down from her stool.

"What seems to be the problem?" Garrett said in a deep commanding voice.

Ellie hurried to his side, grabbing his arm as a growing crowd of people spread out in a wide circle, filling the shop. She gasped when she saw the same four guys who had come into her store to harass her several days ago wandering around inside.

They didn't fit in. It wasn't any one thing, but a collection of parts that made them stand out. All four were dressed in black with black leather boots, black jeans, and black T-shirts. They were in their early twenties she guessed, but it was hard to tell since they had ball caps covering their hair and partially blocking their expressions.

If any one of them had come in and gotten in line for a cupcake, they wouldn't have raised an eyebrow. But they had spread out around the room, and their presence was intimidating people. They were strutting around, touching everything from tables to knickknacks to walls to counters.

A child was crying, and it was her dad who had gotten to his feet and engaged with them. Ellie had no idea what he might have said before she arrived, but she gripped Garrett's arm as the man spoke again. "This is a family shop. Take your bad language and manners and get out of here."

Daddy stuck out an arm to stop Ellie's advance and shot her a sharp look. "Let me handle this," he demanded.

She nodded and took a step back. Her instinct was to jump into the fray and stand up to these hoodlums, but Garrett was right. He was much larger and gruffer than her. She needed to let him deal with the conflict.

Three of the men stood on three sides of the shop, feet planted, hands on their hips, smirks on their faces. One man was facing off with the child's father. He reached out with a foot and kicked over the man's chair. "Fuck you. I have just as much right to be here as you do, asshole."

The man stood taller, taking a step closer, putting himself between his daughter and the thug.

Daddy was bigger than both men, and he advanced quickly. "That's enough." He met the ruffian's gaze and pointed at the door. "You've got three seconds to get out of here, and I don't want to see you anywhere near this strip mall again."

"Or what, old guy?" the man taunted, puffing out his chest and turning his attention toward Garrett.

A silent figure moved to stand at Garrett's side. Bear. He'd promised to come by at some point during the day to see how things were going, and he'd entered Little Cakes with excellent timing. He said nothing but provided another barrier to protect the crowd.

Ellie gasped and gripped the back of the chair in front of her. She had no idea what to do. Tori darted forward and helped the man's crying young daughter from the chair and backed her up away from the conflict as Garrett and Bear backed up the customer.

"I called the police," Lark called from behind the counter. "They're on their way."

"You heard her. The police are on the way. Get out!" Daddy ordered, his gaze darting around at each of the men.

"It's time to get out of here," mumbled one of the aggressors. He quickly jogged to the door and was followed by the other two who'd also remained on the periphery.

The one man who appeared to be the ringleader didn't even glance at his friends as they abandoned him. "Make me."

Daddy didn't hesitate. In the blink of an eye, he grabbed one of the man's arms, twisted it behind his back, and slammed him face first against the wall.

The thug grunted. "Get your fucking hands off me, asshole."

The man struggled, but he was no match for Daddy—especially with Bear standing close to back him up.

Ellie's heart was racing. *How dare this guy ruin my opening day! And why?* She didn't know any of these men. Why were they harassing her cupcake shop for no good reason? She knew they'd also bothered Daisy at her florist shop this week.

Garrett jerked the man's arm up higher against his back and dragged him out the front door. At least he was no longer inside the store, but the fact that her Daddy was still engaged with the man out on the sidewalk made Ellie very nervous.

"It's all over folks. Sorry for the disturbance," Bear reassured the crowd, breaking the tension.

The volume in the room picked up as everyone started whispering about the incident.

When someone touched Ellie's arm, she jerked around to find Riley behind her with a large tray of cut-up pieces of cupcake. "I'll handle things in here so you can go outside and talk to the police, okay?"

Ellie let out a long breath. "Thank you."

"No problem." Riley turned toward the room. "Who wants samples?" It was an excellent idea and the crowd quickly refocused on their favorite cupcake flavors.

Ellie stepped outside as the police pulled up, lights on. Two officers climbed out of the squad car, a man and a woman.

"Garrett," the male officer said as he nodded toward Daddy. He obviously already knew him. "This one of the same thugs who harassed your woman a few days ago?"

"Yes. He had his other friends with him today, too, but they took off running."

The female officer stepped up to face the hooligan. "Hello, Ben."

"How do you know my name, bitch?" the thug shouted, still trying to get away from Garrett's grip.

The woman smirked. "You've been leaving your fingerprints all over the state, Ben, as you vandalized and robbed. The jig is up. You're under arrest." She pulled out her handcuffs while Daddy flattened the man to the side of the building. She continued to read him his rights as he cussed under his breath.

The male officer approached Ellie as the female officer escorted Ben to the back of the squad car. "Are you Ellie Willmoth?"

"Yes." She cleared her throat, noticing her voice was shaky. "I own Little Cakes."

The officer shook her hand and smiled. "Wyatt Hazelton. I'm so sorry you had to deal with this thug on your opening day." He glanced at the shop. "I've heard great things about your cupcakes from Garrett."

Garrett, finally free of Ben, came to her side and set his hand on the back of her neck, pulling her into his chest. He leaned his lips down to her ear. "You okay, Rainbow?" he whispered.

She tipped her head back to look at him. "I think so, Daddy," she responded without thinking. She gasped and jerked her gaze to the officer.

He winked at her and spoke in a soft voice. "Don't worry. Your secret's safe with me."

Ellie was shaking, her nerves overwhelming her.

Daddy wrapped his arm around her and drew her in closer,

his lips on her ear again. "It's okay, Rainbow. Wyatt is a Daddy, too. We go way back. I've known him for years."

Ellie tried to relax in Garrett's arms but it was impossible. Even when he ran his hand up and down her biceps, she still trembled. "Thank you for coming," she managed.

He smiled broadly. "Of course. It's my job. Ben and his cronies have been vandalizing and robbing various shops in several counties for weeks now. I don't think he even tried to avoid getting caught. His fingerprints are everywhere. I found out his prints matched those he left at Daisy's florist shop and finally compared his picture with those at several precincts around the state this morning. I wish I could have caught him sooner."

Ellie forced a smile. "I'm just glad you got him now. What about his friends?"

"I'm sure we'll get all of them in custody soon, but Ben is the ringleader. I don't think the others will show their faces around here again with him in custody," Wyatt assured her.

She hoped he was right. She glanced both ways to find no one was standing close enough to hear her. Nevertheless, she kept her voice low. "Do you have a Little boy or girl at home who would like a cupcake? I'd like to box some up for you as a thank you."

Wyatt smiled. "I don't. Not yet. Still looking for the perfect Little for me. But I won't turn down a cupcake myself. I bet my partner won't, either. We'll pay for them, of course. I was meaning to come by after I got off work today and try out your treats anyway. I'll come back when my shift is over." He winked at her.

Eyes wide, she shook her head. "Oh, no. I couldn't possibly take your money. But I'll save you some of my favorites before they run out."

He grinned. "Appreciate it, little one." He turned and headed for the squad car.

Daddy gave Ellie another squeeze before cupping the sides

of her face and meeting her gaze. "You need a minute? Or do you want to go back inside?"

She took a deep breath. "I think I'm okay. Let's go back inside."

As Ellie let Garrett lead her back into her shop, a huge weight lifted off her shoulders. She felt so incredibly lucky. She'd found the perfect Daddy who loved her and took such good care of her. She was also fortunate he'd been at her store today and able to intervene and keep an ugly situation from possibly escalating into something even uglier.

Ellie wasn't sure what might have happened if Garrett hadn't been strong enough and quick enough to haul that man out of her shop. Ben and his friends might have hurt someone or done serious damage to Little Cakes.

As they entered Little Cakes, the customers inside burst into spontaneous applause.

An elderly woman called over the celebration, "I love seeing the good guys win."

"I can see why someone would want to steal these cupcakes. They're amazing," a young man called out.

The crowd agreed with compliments and raised cupcakes to cheer his assessment. Within seconds, the friendly atmosphere of the shop had been restored. Ellie scanned her new customers, realizing that the experience hadn't driven her business away. It had bonded everyone together. They were invested now in Little Cakes and would support her.

Happy tears gathered in her eyes as she smiled at everyone. When her Daddy ushered her through the shop and into the back room, she didn't resist the opportunity to gather herself. When they were alone, she grabbed his waist and tipped her head way back. "Thank you, Daddy," she murmured. "You're the bestest Daddy in the whole world." She wrapped her arms around him and hugged him as tightly as she could.

Chapter Seventeen

Garrett kept a sharp eye on his Little girl for the rest of the day. She seemed to bounce back and shake off the drama, but he wasn't certain how much she was holding inside. He kept fearing she might be putting on a front.

When Little Cakes finally flipped the sign to closed at seven o'clock, everyone was giddy with excitement. Lark and Ellie jumped up and down hugging each other, but the other employees held as much pride as the two friends for a successful opening day.

"I can't believe how many people came in," Ellie exclaimed.

"We sold out of seven flavors and only have about two dozen cupcakes total left in the back," Riley informed her.

Tori dropped onto a chair and groaned. "My feet are killing me."

Sue sat next to her. "You were amazing with that man's daughter this afternoon. I was relieved when you helped back her out of the way. I was too far away to pull the child to safety."

Tori shrugged. "Instinct, I guess. I was afraid her dad was going to throw a punch, and Lord knows what might have happened if he'd provoked that man."

Lark shuddered. "It helped that Bear happened to stop by with perfect timing. That man is intimidating when he wants to be."

Ellie giggled.

"You all did a fantastic job," Garrett informed them as he pulled his Little girl into his arms, hugging her against his chest. He hoped she wouldn't mind this level of display of affection in front of her employees. He would never do anything to reveal their private relationship to anyone, but it would be too much to ask for him to keep her at arm's length. He needed to touch her. He *wanted* to touch her.

Ellie didn't balk or flinch, which relieved him. In fact, she rose up onto her toes and kissed him in front of everyone. "You were wonderful."

"He really was," Lark agreed. "I think at least ten women in the store swooned when you flattened that thug against the wall." She dramatically ran the back of her hand over her forehead, making everyone laugh.

Garrett rolled his eyes. "I'm not ordinarily fond of violence, but it appeared things might have escalated quickly if someone didn't step in and put an end to the harassment. I knew I would have to act quickly when he flipped the chair."

Ellie released him and faced her employees. "You all can go home. The place is spotless. Thanks for helping clean up in the last hour while customers slowed down to a trickle."

"No problem," Sue and Tori said at the same time.

Everyone gathered their belongings, and Garrett unlocked the front door to let them out before relocking it and turning to find his Little's shoulders dropping in exhaustion. "We need to get you home, get you fed, and spend some time relaxing. How about we veg out in front of a movie before bedtime?"

She smiled, her expression coy. "Maybe..."

He narrowed his brows, unable to keep from grinning. "Did you have something else in mind?"

She let her gaze roam up and down his body, a slow perusal

that made his cock jump to attention. "Do you know how hot it was to watch you manhandle that thug out of my store, Daddy?"

He smirked. "You liked that, huh?"

"Yep. Lark was right. Half the room swooned, myself included. I've been thinking about you manhandling *me* in a similar fashion ever since."

He slowly approached, his gaze pinned on hers. "Is that so?"

"Mmm hmm."

If he wasn't mistaken, she was trembling. Adorably. When he reached her, he took her hand and led her into the back room. He pointed at the work table. "Lean over the top, Rainbow."

She looked at him with wide eyes. "Are you going to spank me?"

He smiled slowly, feeling mischievous at her suggestion. He hadn't thought to spank her right now. He'd only meant to pin her down and reach between her legs to get her off before they went home, but now that she mentioned it...

"I haven't been naughty," she rushed to add as she backed up toward the counter.

He closed the distance and cupped her cheek. "Not all spankings need to be for punishment. Some Littles enjoy a nice spanking for pleasure," he proposed.

She shuddered and then began to fidget. "Oh."

He grinned. "You might like it."

She swallowed hard. "Maybe."

He turned her to angle her over the table and ran his hand over her bottom and thighs, warming her up.

Suddenly, Ellie twisted her face to look at him. "Daddy?"

"Yes, Rainbow?"

She grinned, and while he couldn't imagine what she was going to say next, his heart nearly beat out of his chest at her words. "You told me the next time you spanked me like this, my pants and panties would be down around my ankles." She bit into her lower lip after taunting him with those words.

Garrett leaned over, kissed her cheek, and slid his lips to her ear. "I did, didn't I?" He was beyond pleased with her playfulness, especially considering how tired she had to be.

Rounding to her backside, he reached around, unbuttoned her jeans, lowered the zipper, and tugged the denim as well as her cupcake panties down to her ankles.

His precious Little girl sighed loudly as she relaxed against the table.

Garrett came to her side, lifted her rainbow T-shirt up her back, and held it with one large palm. He smoothed his other hand on her bottom, rubbing it gently for a bit. "You understand this spanking isn't for punishment, right? It's for pleasure this time. Daddy is going to strike you differently and then I'm going to reach between your legs and finger your pussy. You're not to come until I say so though. Understood?"

"Yes, Sir," she managed to breathe out.

The waiting would be the hardest on her. *Whack! Whack! Whack!* Garrett dropped his hand onto her rounded flesh and watched in satisfaction as red handprints appeared. Deep inside, he liked having his mark on her. Ellie was his Little girl.

Her quick inhales of breath captivated him. She was delightful. He cupped her warmed flesh and squeezed slightly.

"Oh! Daddy, I don't like being spanked," Ellie protested as she wiggled.

"If you lie to Daddy, I'll have to spank you more."

"No really! I'm telling the truth!" she swore empathically.

Garrett didn't answer. He just traced the cleft of her bottom with two fingers. When she bucked up from her position lying on the table, he restrained her to the cold surface with his other hand. His probing digits glided into her wetness. Lifting his hand to his mouth, Garrett licked his fingers clean as she watched over her shoulder.

"How many swats should this naughty bottom get for lying

to Daddy, Little girl?" Garrett asked as he returned his fingers to play in the slick juices between her legs.

"No more," she pleaded, squirming under his stimulating touch.

"No more spanks?" he repeated, circling her hidden bundle of nerves. "Then you might think you could always lie to Daddy without earning a consequence."

"I'll never lie again!" she promised.

"I don't believe you, Little girl. Just as you weren't to orgasm until I gave you permission," he reminded her as he stroked her intimately.

Panting, she met his gaze. "I haven't!"

Garrett pinched her clit and watched her mouth open in a silent scream as obvious pleasure exploded within her. His fingers moved slowly through her pink folds to sustain her orgasm as he unfastened his jeans and lifted himself free of the confinement.

"Daddy?" she asked, panting against the metal worktable. "I didn't mean to come. You made me."

"No excuses for bad behavior, Little girl. The consequences have now increased."

He watched as her eyes seem to regain their ability to focus and she looked back to see what he was suggesting. Garrett stroked down his cock to cradle his heavy balls in his hand. "I'm going to be here," he explained in a husky voice.

Pressing three of his fingers together, he held them steady at her sensitive entrance. Her palms flattened against the table as he slid them slowly into her tight passage. Garrett held his hand tight against her body, enjoying the feel of her muscles pulling him inside.

Unable to resist the allure of her body, Garrett released his penis and reached for his wallet. Setting it near her hands, he directed, "Open Daddy's wallet. Find the condom."

Slapping her bottom when she didn't move fast enough,

Garrett simultaneously moved his inserted hand to stroke out of her body and back in firmly. "Condom," he reminded her.

Immediately, she grabbed the wallet and unfolded it. He continued to spank her bottom and stimulate her as she searched for the condom tucked inside. Her fingers closed on the crinkling packet, and she pulled it out. She ripped it open with her teeth, pulled the rolled barrier out, and waved it toward him.

"Here, Daddy. Oh, please! Here!"

Garrett pulled his dripping fingers from her body and spanked her red bottom one last time with his wet digits, loving the sight of her juices smeared on her skin as proof of her desire. After rolling the condom over his cock, he placed the head against her body and pressed inward. He could feel the heat of her punished skin as he drew close and ground his pelvis against hers to remind her of her spanking.

"Please!" she wailed.

Gripping her hips, Garrett thrust in and out of her body, building the passion between them. Ellie rose to her toes to press her bottom against him as her mouth fell open. He intensified his pace as her tight channel pulsed around him.

"Can I come?" she pleaded.

"Count backward from ten," he commanded.

"What?"

"Ten," he began, grinding against her.

"Nine?" she struggled to say after a few seconds and a couple strong strokes. "Eight! Seven! Six!"

Her eyes closed as he moved against her. A few seconds passed and he spanked her bottom sharply, reminding her, "Count!"

"Five! Four! Three! Two! One!" Ellie speed-talked in a slur of words as Garrett moved at lightning speed.

He emptied himself into the condom as she cried out. Garrett sank to his forearms on either side of her shaking body, holding himself deeper inside her. He kissed her sensitive neck, whispering praise.

"You are my precious Little, Ellie. Daddy is very proud of you."

"I love you, Daddy."

"I love you, too, Rainbow."

His mouth captured hers. Garrett's tender kiss expressed all his passion and special feelings for Ellie. Eventually, he forced himself to withdraw. It was time to take his Little girl home.

When he had redressed them both and had Ellie belted securely in his SUV, Garrett started the engine and headed for his house. He paused to watch her curl up in the bucket seat. His Little leaned her head against his forearm on the padded armrest on the console. He ran his fingers through her hair to brush it from her face before shifting into drive.

"Daddy?"

"Yes, Rainbow?"

"Can I have more soup? You know, in the bottle?"

"Absolutely."

Chapter Eighteen

The next morning, Ellie yawned as her Daddy drove her back to the shop. She was eager to start the day and knew there would be a lot of cupcakes to concoct. Crossing her fingers, she hoped she had enough sprinkles to decorate a bunch.

She'd woken up in the middle of the night and worried. Her Daddy had heard her through the baby monitor and had come in to check on her. Talking to her softly, he'd helped her fill her diaper. Once changed, he'd tucked her in the crib and had rubbed her back until Ellie had fallen back to sleep.

As they walked up to the back door, she noticed a large package. "What's that?"

"An overnight delivery from the grocery store," he explained, hefting it into his arms.

She had him set it on the table and felt her cheeks warm. Ellie'd never look at that workspace again without blushing. Busying herself with opening the box, she tried to ignore his knowing chuckle. Spreading the flaps of the carton, she discovered that it was packed full of small jars of rainbow sprinkles.

"Did you buy every sprinkle in town?"

"I tried."

Unable to believe how lucky she was to find this incredible

man, Ellie rushed forward to wrap her arms around his hard torso. He hugged her back just as tightly. Rising on her tiptoes, Ellie pressed her lips against his, feeling the passion combust between them.

"Whoa! There needs to be more cooking and less kissing in here." Bear's deep voice made her dance away from her Daddy.

When her eyes guiltily focused on the table before them, the large baker added, "And we obviously need to disinfect surfaces before we start today."

"Good idea," Garrett agreed without a speck of discretion.

"Daddy!" Ellie protested, feeling her face heat even more. She slapped her hands over her cheeks.

Bear took pity on her. "I'm going to do a quick inventory." He disappeared into the walk-in cooler with a pad of paper and a pen.

"You!" Ellie waggled her finger at Garrett. "Go away and let me focus. You are too big of a distraction."

"Give me a kiss first and I'll be gone," Garrett instructed as he swept her into his arms.

Ellie lifted her puckered mouth to meet his.

"You're still kissing?" Bear laughed as he exited the storage area.

"I'm on my way out. Make her take a break, Bear," Garrett requested.

"Will do!" came the immediate reply.

"Stop ganging up on me. Out!" She shooed Garrett out the door as she laughed at the two Daddies.

With the door locked, Ellie returned to unpack the box and stow the cardboard in the recycling bin. As she wiped down all the surfaces with a warm face, she conferred with Bear over the state of their supplies. Within minutes, the whirl of the large table mixers and the blowers on the preheating ovens created the background sounds that were music to her ears. Thank goodness Bear was able to come in again this morning. If the shop remained as busy as it had on the first day, she'd need him every night, not just three nights a week.

A few minutes before they were supposed to open, Lark burst through the kitchen door, looking over her shoulder, and almost running into Bear as he carried a fresh tray of rainbow sprinkled cupcakes for the display counter.

"Whoa, Little girl," he breathed, balancing the teetering tray while steadying Lark with a hand on her shoulder.

Ellie watched with growing wonder. Could her friend be Little, too?

"Ellie! That police officer is here. He'd like to talk to you," Lark reported, looking agitated.

"Is something wrong?" Ellie asked as she turned off the mixer. Lark was always composed and professional. She'd never seen her so rattled.

"I don't know," Lark answered. "You come talk to him." She rushed back to the front of the shop.

"Okay."

Wiping her hands on her apron automatically, Ellie walked through the swinging door. The patrolman stood with his back to the kitchen. She followed his line of sight to see him looking at Lark as she tidied the tables. The dangling apron strings swayed over her friend's pert bottom as Lark unnecessarily cleaned the already spotless tables. There seemed to be a bit more enthusiastic movement than necessary.

Okay, it can't be anything too terrible, Ellie decided if he was so distracted. She glanced around to find the rest of her staff grinning. They apparently noticed the odd interaction between Lark and the police officer, too.

"Officer Hazelton, is something wrong?" Ellie asked, breaking the silence.

The handsome man in uniform turned with a smile. "Hi,

161

Ms. Willmoth. No, nothing is wrong. I actually have good news today. We were able to round up the other three men that caused the disruption here."

"Really? They're behind bars?" Ellie asked as her shoulders relaxed from their tensed position.

"They are. There's enough evidence against them all. They should be locked up until their trial date."

"That's incredible news. Da... Garrett will be so happy to hear this," Ellie cheered, catching herself just before she called Garrett, Daddy.

There was a collective sigh of relief in the room.

"That doesn't mean you should stop being vigilant. I teach self-defense classes for women. They're free every month at the police academy. Everyone is welcome," he offered, turning slightly to look back at Lark. When he found her watching, he nodded that upward macho way some men did.

Turning back around, he pulled a card holder out of his pocket. After removing several cards, he handed Ellie a small stack. "Feel free to invite anyone you'd like. Get a group together and come. If you have five or more, I'll give up a day off to offer a private class."

"We might just take you up on that, Officer," Ellie answered.

"Call me Wyatt. This is my normal patrol area. I think I'll stop in often to have a sugar boost."

"You are welcome anytime, Wyatt. I go by Ellie. That's Lark, my amazing friend who's here helping us for a few days. And Sue, Tori, and Riley, along with Bear, make up my staff. You already met Bear. He's in the kitchen."

Her lips curled up as she watched Wyatt walk deliberately to Lark's side to hand her one of his cards. Their gazes met and Ellie could feel the sizzle of heat between them. The normally unflappable realtor's cheeks turned rosy as she dropped her attention to the small rectangle of paper in her hand.

Smiling, Wyatt excused himself. "I'll see you all soon."

He was almost to the door when Lark called, "Would you and your partner like a cupcake?"

"Not this time, thank you." Wyatt patted his slim, hard stomach, drawing all their attention to his lower half. "I don't want to have to run extra laps tonight. Next time, for sure."

This time as he turned to leave, Ellie noticed all the ladies staring at his toned butt. As much as she wanted people to devour her cupcakes, who wouldn't enjoy Wyatt's dedicated fitness goals?

When the bells at the door jingled closed, Ellie teased her friend, "Lark and Wyatt, sitting in a tree. K-I-S-S-I-N-G!"

"Stop it! He's not interested in me," Lark protested, turning a bit pinker.

"Oh, he likes you. I'm sure you could get some private lessons," Riley suggested.

"You guys!" Lark protested. Dramatically, she glanced at her watch. "Oh, look at the time. I have to go. I'm taking a client to see some new houses in the area."

"Thanks for stopping by to check on us, Lark. Want a cupcake for the road?" Ellie asked, grabbing a to-go container.

"Yes! They're so good. Rainbow Sprinkles, please. I have to try the cupcake that launched Little Cakes!"

When Ellie brought her the box, Lark handed Ellie her apron and gave her friend a big hug. "You're doing so well." She paused just a second before whispering in Ellie's ear, "Do you think he really likes me?"

"I'd bet a lifetime supply of sprinkles," Ellie assured her.

"Wow! I'm going to have to think about this."

"You do that. Now, scoot. Off to your meeting. I'll see you soon, I'm sure," Ellie said, giving her one last squeeze.

"That was interesting. Did you feel the heat as he got close to her?" Tori asked after the door jingled closed behind Lark. "I hope someone yummy comes in and scoops me up."

Everyone turned to look at the quiet, efficient woman. She didn't usually jump into the conversations between the women.

Before anyone could respond, the door opened and a mom and ten teenagers walked in. They were officially open. Time to get to work.

"It's my turn to feed these guys after practice. They're starving. Guys, pick a couple of cupcakes and get some milk," she directed, herding the uniformed, sweaty teens toward the counter with an apologetic smile towards the ladies who rushed into position to help them.

Soon, the room resounded with excited chatter and moans of delight at the yummy cupcakes. They ended up each eating three or four cupcakes. The mother allowed them to eat their fill and requested a dozen to take home with her for her husband and daughter to try. She didn't blink at the total but handed over her credit card with a smile.

"If everyone likes your treats as well as these guys, you're going to sell millions of cupcakes!"

Chapter Nineteen

Ellie cuddled against her Daddy as they sat on the couch after dinner. She yawned as the cartoon on the screen faded away. Her bedtime had been in effect for a few weeks. Although she hated to admit it, Ellie did feel better having a regular sleep cycle. Going to bed was hard because she didn't want to leave her Daddy.

"It's almost time to put Cuddles and Sprinkles in the crib, Little girl."

"Five more minutes, Daddy?"

"We have just enough time to rock before bed. Let's head to your nursery."

Garret stood and tugged Ellie to her feet. Wrapping his arm around her waist, he guided her into the beautiful room.

"It's not really *my* nursery, Daddy. I just keep staying here." Ellie peeked up at him, trying to read his reaction to her words. She'd felt like she was straddling two worlds—part time Little, part time Big.

Garrett had transported a lot of Ellie's clothing and possessions to his house. The closet in the nursery was filled with her clothes and shoes. The master closet now housed her jewelry and other precious possessions. Her apartment was virtually empty.

Garrett frowned. "Of course, it's your nursery, Rainbow. I think we'll paint a rainbow on that wall over there. Then, you'll know this is your home."

Tears welled in her eyes, blinding her. Ellie stopped in the middle of the room and covered her face. She so wanted this to be her real home. It would be a fairy tale come true if her Daddy had found her and wanted to keep her. Overwhelmed, she sobbed, already anticipating the day Garrett would decide she wasn't worth being his.

Instantly, his warm arms wrapped around her. Her Daddy swept her up in his arms and carried her to the large rocking chair. She turned to bury her face against him as he cradled her against his hard, strong body. When he sat down and pushed with his feet to move the chair, she sobbed even harder.

"Little girl. You're breaking my heart. I don't think you've figured out that I'm keeping you forever."

"This can't last. People don't get to live as Littles. I'm going to miss you so much." Muffled by his shirt, Ellie pushed out the words between sobs from her hiding spot under his jaw.

Scared he would think she was too needy, Ellie covered her mouth with one hand to stifle the sound and tried to force herself to stop crying. *Enough! He's going to send me back to that lonely apartment.*

"Rainbow, you're going to make yourself sick." His hands stroked down her back to pat her bottom. "I will spank you if that's what it takes to get your attention."

When she shook her head against him, he stroked up her spine and rubbed back and forth over her ribcage. "Breathe with me. In," he commanded, audibly inhaling and lifting her body slightly as his chest rose.

After a split-second pause, she followed his directions.

"Good girl. Out." Garrett again guided her with an exaggerated exhale. He continued to breathe with her as if he had all the time in the world.

Slowly, Ellie felt herself relax against his chest. Tears still leaked from her eyes, but her heart rate slowed from the earlier panicked flutter. "I'm so silly."

"You absolutely are not. This is one hundred percent my fault. I am very sorry." His voice was husky with emotion.

Surprised, Ellie sat up to look at his face. A slow tear slid from the corner of his eye to disappear in his thick hair. "Don't cry, Daddy," she urged, reaching one suspiciously damp hand forward to wipe away the moisture.

"I have not taken care of you as I should have, Rainbow. Daddies get scared sometimes, too. I hoped you would decide that this was the place you wanted to stay. It's my fault that I didn't talk to you directly."

"You get scared, too?"

"Losing you frightens me the most. You stole part of my heart at our first meeting as you danced and baked like no one was watching."

"No one was supposed to be watching, Daddy," she reminded him, feeling her cheeks warm.

His hand cupped her cheek. "I found you absolutely adorable then. And I find you even more desirable now. Being your Daddy, taking care of you, and nurturing your Little is all I want to do. It's all I've ever wanted."

"You take very good care of me."

"I let the uncertainty make you unhappy. How about if I tell you exactly how I see my future?"

"O... Okay." She stumbled over the word.

"You move the rest of your stuff into the basement or a storage area and live full-time with me for the rest of your life."

"That sounds like a very long commitment."

"Forever, Little girl. I love you and want my Little girl with me. Could you see yourself happy here?"

"Are we going to get married?"

"If you'd like. I'll propose now if you want. I love you, Ellie Willmoth."

"I love you, too, Daddy."

Ellie threw herself forward to press a million kisses on his face. "I don't care if we get married. I just want to be with you."

"Then, we close up your apartment this weekend and give your notice. You won't be able to walk to work from my house. I'll make sure you get there every day and pick you up. Or we can get you a safe car to drive if you need to be independent," he suggested, arching one eyebrow.

Giggling at his silly face, Ellie shook her head. "I hate driving. Besides, that's your job as a Daddy, right?"

"Right," he confirmed with a nod. "Daddies take care of their Littles however they need to be looked after."

She leaned forward to press her mouth against his in a tender kiss filled with all the emotions swirling around inside her. Lifting her head, she stared at him, trying to see if there were any signs of doubt in his mind.

Reading her mind, Garrett dispelled any lingering negative thoughts haunting her brain. "I'm not going to change my mind. You're mine, Little girl. Besides, you make good naked cupcakes. I have to keep you around. No one else makes them."

"Those sell like hot cakes to the yoga ladies when they come out of the studio next door!" Ellie squirmed slightly on top of him as she got excited.

"Shh, Little girl. No plotting world cupcake domination before bedtime. That can wait until you get to the store tomorrow. Here, you're my precious Rainbow."

His stern voice wiped all the zinging thoughts from her mind. Ellie laid her head on his shoulder and breathed with him. Nestling her nose against him, she inhaled the fresh manly scent that was her Daddy's alone. As the chair rocked smoothly below her, the familiar routine soothed and relaxed her.

A large yawn stretched her mouth wide. Settling happily into place, she patted her Daddy's chest. "My Daddy."

His lips pressed against her temple. "Your Daddy."

As he rose from the rocking chair, cradling her in his arms, she tipped her head back to look at him. She didn't want him to put her to bed in her crib tonight. She wanted to remain snuggled in his arms. "Can I sleep with you in your bed tonight, Daddy?"

He smiled at her before bopping her nose. For a moment she thought he would tell her that Little girls needed to sleep in their own cribs, but he surprised her. "I'd like that, Rainbow. I'd like that a lot."

She knew her grin stretched from ear to ear.

"But..." he added, making her heart rate pick up, "you'll have to get to bed on an earlier schedule on the nights you sleep with Daddy." He gave her a mischievous grin that made her squirm in his arms.

"Why, Daddy?" she asked, blinking innocently.

He chuckled as he turned to head for the hallway. "Keep squirming like that and you'll find out exactly why, my little Rainbow."

Ellie giggled all the way to his room, but she didn't stop squirming. No way.

Here's a sneak peak at the next book in the Little Cakes Series: Lemon Chiffon.

"Hey, Dungeon Master. I've got a new whiskey for you to sample," Riley called across the social gathering area of Blaze.

"I don't drink while I'm on duty," he answered curtly. She knew that was the rule.

"At least come sniff this. You'll want to come back after your shift is over." She coaxed him to approach.

"Sniff it?" Bear shook his head as he walked her way. Had Riley been drinking too much? That wasn't like her at all. As he approached, she waved him around the bar.

"Careful. Don't look down," Riley whispered to him from the corner of her mouth as she held the bottle toward his nose.

"Check this out," she announced louder for the crowd gathered around the bar.

Instantly, Bear's warning radar sounded. Something wasn't right here. As he dipped his head to sniff, Bear saw a huddled figure pressed as small as possible against the wooden barrier.

"Teddy?" A small sound whispered from the back of the bar. "Can you get me out of here? I'm scared."

Daisy! The nickname the Littles didn't think he knew about clued him in as to how frightened she had to be. He dropped a hand down to stroke over her silky hair to reassure her. Bear didn't stop to question why she was hiding. The Little had a good reason.

"That smells amazing, Riley. I'll look forward to sampling it soon."

Bear walked to the supply cabinet and grabbed a folded black tablecloth. Nonchalantly walking back to the bar, he searched for a way to create a distraction. A flash of movement captured his attention as Blaze's resident shibari expert appeared. Milo's rope demonstrations were extremely popular.

"Hey, Knot Master! When's the next performance? Weren't you looking for volunteers?" Bear sacrificed the experienced member to the eager crowd. He'd apologize later.

As everyone swarmed to speak to Milo, Bear wrapped the tablecloth around Daisy and carried her into the office unseen. Sitting down in the large chair, he freed the small figure from the material. The sight of her tear-stained face thrust a stake through his heart. Instantly, he was ready to pounce on whoever had hurt her.

"Teddy!" Daisy threw herself against his chest and wrapped her arms around his neck, holding on tightly. "I knew you'd help me!"

Author's Note

We hope you're enjoying Little Cakes! We are so excited to be working together to create this new series! More stories will be coming soon!

Little Cakes:
(by Pepper North and Paige Michaels)
Rainbow Sprinkles
Lemon Chiffon
Blue Raspberry
Red Velvet
Pink Lemonade
Black Forest
Witch's Brew
Pumpkin Spice
Santa's Kiss
Fudge Crunch
Sweet Tooth
Flirty Kumquat
Birthday Cake
Caramel Drizzle

Maraschino Cherry
Reindeer Tracks

About Pepper North

Ever just gone for it? That's what *USA Today* Bestselling Author Pepper North did in 2017 when she posted a book for sale on Amazon without telling anyone. Thanks to her amazing fans, the support of the writing community, Mr. North, and a killer schedule, she has now written more than 70 books!

Enjoy contemporary, paranormal, dark, and erotic romances that are both sweet and steamy? Pepper will convert you into one of her loyal readers. What's coming in the future? A Daddypalooza!

Connect with me on your favorite platform!
I'm also having fun on TikTok as well!

amazon.com/author/pepper_north
bookbub.com/profile/pepper-north
facebook.com/AuthorPepperNorth
instagram.com/4peppernorth
pinterest.com/4peppernorth
twitter.com/@4peppernorth

Pepper North Series

Dr. Richards' Littles®

A beloved age play series that features Littles who find their forever Daddies and Mommies. Dr. Richards guides and supports their efforts to keep their Littles happy and healthy.

Available on Amazon

SANCTUM

Pepper North introduces you to an age play community that is isolated from the surrounding world. Here Littles can be Little, and Daddies can care for their Littles and keep them protected from the outside world.

Available on Amazon

Soldier Daddies

What private mission are these elite soldiers undertaking? They're all searching for their perfect Little girl.

Available on Amazon

The Keepers

This series from Pepper North is a twist on contemporary age play romances. Here are the stories of humans cared for by specially selected Keepers of an alien race. These are science fiction novels that age play readers will love!

Available on Amazon

The Magic of Twelve

The Magic of Twelve features the stories of twelve women transported on their 22nd birthday to a new life as the droblin (cherished Little one) of a Sorcerer of Bairn. These magic wielders have waited a long time to take complete care of their droblin's needs. They will protect their precious one to their last drop of magic from a growing menace. Each novel is a complete story.

Available on Amazon

About Paige Michaels

Paige Michaels is a USA Today bestselling author of naughty romance books that are meant to make you squirm. She loves a happily ever after and spends the bulk of every day either reading erotic romance or writing it.

Other books by Paige Michaels:

The Nurturing Center:
Susie
Emmy
Jenny
Lily
Annie
Mindy

Eleadian Mates:
His Little Emerald
His Little Diamond
His Little Garnet
His Little Amethyst
His Little Sapphire
His Little Topaz

Littleworld:
Anabel's Daddy
Melody's Daddy

Haley's Daddy
Willow's Daddy
Juliana's Daddy
Tiffany's Daddy
Felicity's Daddy
Emma's Daddy
Lizzy's Daddy
Claire's Daddy
Kylie's Daddy
Ruby's Daddy
Briana's Daddies
Jake's Mommy and Daddy
Luna's Daddy
Petra's Daddy
Littleworld Box Set One
Littleworld Box Set Two
Littleworld Box Set Three
Littleworld Box Set Four

Holidays at Rawhide Ranch:
Felicity's Little Father's Day
A Cheerful Little Coloring Day

If you'd like to see a map of Regression island where Littleworld
is located, please visit my website: PaigeMichaels.com

facebook.com/PaigeMichaelsAuthor
amazon.com/author/PaigeMichaels
bookbub.com/authors/paige-michaels

Afterword

If you've enjoyed this story, it will make our day if you could leave an honest review on Amazon. Reviews help other people find our books and help us continue creating more Little adventures. Our thanks in advance. We always love to hear from our readers what they enjoy and dislike when reading an alternate love story featuring age-play.

Made in United States
Orlando, FL
24 August 2023

36381116R00104